W9-BEU-563

THE
SIN
EATER

THE
SIN
EATER

Gary D. Schmidt

Lodestar Books
Dutton   New York

No character in this book is intended to represent any actual person; all the incidents of the story are entirely fictional in nature.

Copyright © 1996 by Gary D. Schmidt

Library of Congress Cataloging-in-Publication Data

Schmidt, Gary D.
   The sin eater / Gary D. Schmidt.
      p.   cm.
   Summary: While living on his grandparents' farm in New Hampshire, Cole hears stories about a mysterious Sin Eater; these stories enable Cole to learn forgiveness and to connect with his ancestors.
   ISBN 0-525-67541-8
   [1. Grandparents—Fiction.   2. Farm life—New Hampshire— Fiction.   3. Death—Fiction.   4. New Hampshire—Fiction.]
   I. Title.
PZ7.S3527Si   1996
[Fic]—dc20   96-14372   CIP   AC

Published in the United States by Lodestar Books,
an affiliate of Dutton Children's Books,
a division of Penguin Books USA Inc.,
375 Hudson Street, New York, New York 10014

Published simultaneously in Canada
by McClelland & Stewart, Toronto

Editor: Virginia Buckley   Designer: Marilyn Granald

Printed in the U.S.A.   First Edition   10 9 8 7 6 5 4 3 2 1

for Margaret and Benjamin,
for whom the stories are just beginning

The Sin Eater

Some still recall the days of the Sin Eaters, especially in the Welsh villages far from the sea where stone cottages cling to the hills and people hold to their ways. The Sin Eater followed hurt and death. If it was hurt, the kind of hurt that wounded the soul, then the Sin Eater came by night to collect the bread left as an offering to him. Its yeast was the pain of the baker. The Sin Eater took it, silently, into himself.

But if it was death, mourning families summoned the Sin Eater from the edge of the wilderness to eat the bread kneaded through and through with the sins of their dear one, bread still warm with its baking, placed by a loving hand on the chest of the corpse. And when the Sin Eater took the loaf and ate it, no one gave him thanks and no one wanted to remember him. They threw a coin, then stones, until he ran, carrying his awful load of someone else's sin, coming at last to the wild, lonely place he lived.

Behind him, the Sin Eater left dancing and singing.

I first heard of the Sin Eaters long after their time, on

the spring night before we buried Ma. I think it was spring. It was still winter cold, like it had been since before Christmas, when Ma heard back from the doctor with the report that froze our life still. Dad and I decorated a tree and made it through the holiday, but mostly we just watched as the cancer slowly, and then more and more quickly, gobbled up Ma's life from the inside and left us all three dying a little bit more every day. We left the woodstove cold and used propane to keep the house hotter than summer, but we walked around shivering all through January, February, and into March, when the sap started to run in the sugar maples and Ma's sweet life leaked away until she was still forever.

"She should be with her people," Grandpa said when Dad called, and so we brought her home to New Hampshire.

The night we arrived, Grandma baked bread. I helped her knead the dough and punch down its rising, the flour like dust up my arms. Grandpa watched us from the kitchen table, and when Grandma set the brown and steaming loaves by him, he took her by the elbow, brushed her hair with the back of his fingers, and said, his smile quivering, "No Sin Eater tonight. There isn't any need. Not for her." And reaching down they gathered me into them and we held one another, shaking, against the spinning world.

Now I know they were wrong about the Sin Eater. There was need. But if there had still been one in Albion, New Hampshire, it wouldn't have been for Ma that he came. He would have come for us. And he might have left a dance and a song behind him.

ONE

THE LAST DAY OF SCHOOL was my last day in Pennsylvania. I spent it setting memories down deep, sharp and focused so that they wouldn't blur: friends I had for eight years of homerooms. The long, right-angled halls now filled with lockers yawing open and spilling broken-backed books, last October's spelling lists, torn hall passes—the wreckage of a whole year. The smell of the June sun on the white sidewalks, the soft squish of the asphalt I toed up while waiting by the curb, the hard edges of the cracked vinyl bus seats, the hollers celebrating summer—I set them all down deep. I wanted to remember.

My stop. The hollering quieted. "Bye, Cole." "See ya." "Good-bye." I was already more than half gone from their lives.

Dad had the car running in the driveway. I threw my pack in the backseat and climbed in next to him. No need to go in the house: Everything was gone, sold in a hurricane of a garage sale so quickly that my posters had been torn from the walls before I'd gotten them off. Most of my stuff was packed into the car trunk, but we carried nothing else from our old life. "It's best to start over again," Dad had said while taking down the lithographs

1

Ma had framed and hung in the stairwell. They had been the first things to whirl out of our lives in the garage sale.

But there was one thing that I saved. The night before the sale, I snuck into Ma's study. There, on the bottom shelf where it had been forever, I found the copy of *The House at Pooh Corner* that Ma had read to me every night, even past when I was too old to be read to. I peeled off the price tag that the agent had glued to the spine, brought it up to bed, and listened to Ma's voice read to me as I turned the pages. Then I packed it in my suitcase.

Dad backed the car out and headed for Route 276. It had been two years since we last took the trip to New Hampshire. Two years we had stuck it out together, in a hushed life. Before, the house had always been full with the slick and sliding notes of Dad's trombone practice, his notes running their brassy selves up and down scales and then falling, mellow and gold, into long, slow pools of music. He would practice the sets he'd be playing in Philadelphia with his jazz quartet on the weekends, and when he finished, Ma would put on the Cole Porter discs and they'd sit together on the couch, their feet pressed against each other, working out lyrics and melodies and probably wondering why their son didn't have a single note of music in his hands.

After Ma died, Dad kept going in to Philadelphia on the weekends; his schedule had been set through the spring and summer and the quartet told him they needed him, that it would be good for him to get back to work. But he never touched his trombone around the house anymore, and the Cole Porter discs broke into bright shards and were whisked away.

After school, I'd come home to a house perfectly clean, and there would be a perfectly healthy snack waiting for me, and later we would have a perfectly proper dinner. The clink of our forks sounded loud in the dining room. When we were done, Dad washed up and put perfectly clean plates away into perfectly ordered cabinets.

"Aren't you two doing well, considering?" people at church said to us.

"Perfectly," Dad replied. Then we drove home in silence to silence.

Ma haunted the house, not because she was somehow there, but because she was so awfully not there. I half expected to see her every morning when I first opened my eyes. And when I walked in the back door after school I almost always had something to tell her—until the clean emptiness of the kitchen reminded me.

So we decided to move to Albion to tend Ma's grave, to get away from the haunting, and to live. In all that time we hadn't come back to New Hampshire, mostly because we had never been there without Ma. But Dad began to talk of it more and more in between our long silences. It would be good to live in a small town. It would be good to get to know my grandparents better. It would be good to be near my roots. It would be good to be there in case . . . well, in case anything happened. He repeated "would be goods" like he was trying to convince me. But I wasn't the one who needed convincing.

Traffic on 276 was slow, families heading out to the Jersey coast. They'd swim, build castles, eat sandy food, get sunburned, and then drive home to everything that was familiar. Me, I was praying that at least in Albion

3

nothing had changed, not even the little things. I prayed that the cracks in the sidewalks were the same, that the buildings were still painted white and peeling in the same places under the same hot sun, that the bark on the sycamores would scrape as roughly on my palms, that the sky would be as high and as blue and as forever as it always had been.

And I prayed that, on Grandpa's farm, everything would be the same as it had been for as far back as I could remember. I prayed that the clapboard house would be there and the screen door would smack against the pane and the woodstove would shelve rhubarb jars and the steps to the shed would still be as worn and the calendar from Paarlberg Realty would be up and I would stand on the edge of the porch, at the very top of Cobb's Hill, and be able to see far away into Vermont and the cows would still smell of sweet hay and Grandma of lavender water and it would all be the same.

I prayed that in the morning Dad would blast notes from his trombone so that they careened off the maples and scattered into the bright fields to wake the sun. And he would beat Grandma down to the kitchen—or try to— and fluff up two dozen pancakes heavy with blueberries picked during last night's sunset and we would go to chores licking the syrup off our fingers and it would all be the same.

Up until the last two years, I had spent every summer of my life on that farm. I spent my days walking behind Grandpa, or up with him on the tractor, or holding on for dear life to the two-handled saw as Grandpa drew it back and forth back across a downed apple tree. Grandpa's three milkers—Emily, Anne, and Charlotte—were long since past giving milk, but I still had the faintest memory of milking time. Grandpa's hands were over mine on the udder, and my face was pressed against the warm roughness of Emily. Or maybe it was Charlotte. "Back yer leg," Grandpa had growled, and I wasn't sure if he meant me or the cow. But then his voice gentled. "Tuck your thumbs into your palms, Cole, like this. No, like this. That's right. Tuck 'em in. Now pull strong and smooth down into the pail. Strong and smooth. Strong and smooth." And the creamy warmth had come out from under our hands and drained *ching, ching* into the pail.

I prayed about the farm when we turned onto Interstate 95 and headed north, pressing my cheek against the cool of the window and watching New Jersey, New York, Massachusetts, pass by. I wished I was in the backseat. I should be in the backseat, Ma up front. Once we hit Interstate 93 and crossed into New Hampshire, we should all of us be looking for the landmarks that showed we were closing in on Albion. Dad should be calling them out and Ma laughing because he was calling them before he could possibly see them. And I should be counting off the miles left between us and Albion.

But for this trip, I hadn't calculated the miles, and neither of us called out any landmarks. Everything began to look exactly the same for mile after mile. The same green signs announced the same anonymous rest stops. The corn fields, browner than usual for late June, looked like they had been planted by the same farmer, perfect row after perfect row, until I began to wish that someone had let the tractor slip just a bit. The scarred hills, naked where the lanes had torn through them, each had the same warning about falling rocks. And the white lines on the road ribboned on like they had no business doing anything else.

We ate at a place that served roast beef sandwiches with meat that had been dead an awful long time. Ma had always packed a lunch, and we would celebrate getting into the mountains with chicken sandwiches (lots of mayonnaise) on home-baked bread, hard-boiled eggs, long wedges of cucumbers that had come up early from our garden, and tomatoes that we ate like apples.

We had always stopped at the same rest stop and eaten at the same picnic table. After lunch, I had always rolled down the hill and waded into the creek that bubbled and gurgled and did everything it could to let me know how happy it was to see me again. The crayfish would amble up, begging to be caught, and the minnows would swim laps around my shins. Afterwards, when I came back up the hill, the lunch would have been packed away and Ma and Dad would stand there, watching me climb, holding hands and raising their faces together to the fresh breezes that tumbled off the cliffs of the White Mountains.

Outside the roast beef place, the asphalt was hot under our feet. The inside of the car was baking and smelled like burnt popcorn, even though we had left the front windows partway open.

A hundred miles spun underneath our tires before we talked. Dad cleared his throat once, twice. A long pause. Another throat-clearing. I waited for him.

"You know, Cole, it won't be so bad living there."

Ahead of us, a hawk was riding the wind, circling to kill.

"You always liked Albion in summers, and Grandpa's farm. And all."

I nodded. A long pause.

"Driving up here," he said slowly, "it brings it all back. It brings her all back. I know we haven't talked much about your mother. About her being gone. Maybe we should have."

"We still can. She's not gone as long as we can remember her."

He shook his head. "That's the sort of stuff people say in movies, Cole. It's not true. She's gone. People said that the hardest thing about this would be that I would start to forget. First the little things, and then . . . well, and then maybe even how she spoke, how she smelled, what she looked like. But I remember everything. Everything. And what hurts is that I can't be with her anymore." His hands were tight on the wheel. "She's gone, all right."

I looked at him, startled, and my throat tightened.

More miles spinning underneath our tires. More green signs and flowing white lines.

"You're so much like her," Dad said quietly, as though there had been no pause. "Every day that goes by, you remind me of her in a hundred ways. Your eyes. The way you hold your head. The way you chew your pencil when you're thinking. The way you look at something and see exactly what she would have seen. The way you pray at supper to . . . someone you think is really there." He stopped, and took a deep breath. "Maybe that's why it sometimes hurts so much to be around you. Because you're you and not her."

I hunched into myself and tried to keep the pain that

filled my throat from falling sick and sour into my stomach. I closed my eyes against what might happen. Dad turned on the radio, and soon the hum of the tires and the whining of a lonesome singer singing out his lonesome blues became one sound and faded as I fell asleep.

I woke when the car geared down onto the streets of Albion. Too bad, since I'd missed my favorite part of the trip: the climb into the mountains where the trees grow older and thicker and darker, the rocks more jagged—like they'd just been chiseled out and stood bristling at the sunlight. And then suddenly, without a single sign, without so much as a how-do-you-do, there would be the town, stuck against the side of the mountain like it was surprised at itself and holding on for dear life.

Some prayers are answered: Nothing had changed in Albion since I'd last seen it. Every house on the street leading to the Commons had its front painted white, its sides left pretty much alone. The houses around the Commons were all brick, most of them three-stories from the days when Albion had been a lumbering hub and lumbermen made modest fortunes and built immodest houses. Filigree decorated all the wrought-iron fences that ran around the square, and small iron pineapples marked boundary lines between them. They shone dully in the summer heat. Elm stumps were still kneeing up the sidewalks beyond the fences. The smell of newly opened petunias was in the air.

On the next street over from the Commons, the five-and-dime still had its windows crammed with rakes and blue plastic pools and lawn chairs and pet supplies. And across the way, Roy Lanier's Hardware countered with a shiny red rototiller. It had been in that window every summer I could remember but was kept polished, just in case someone might want to buy it. Pelletier's Stationery was closed, though; not everything would be the same.

But Kaye's was still open, and we stopped for our traditional black-and-white sodas. Kaye had gone continental, sticking a white table out front with a broad yellow parasol. But no one was sitting there. No one in Albion would ever sit under a yellow parasol. It was being cleaned by a kid up on a stepladder. I'd seen him once or twice during summers, but I could tell he couldn't make me out: The light reflected off the parasol and he had to squint against the glare. He brushed away what pigeons had left behind and lifted a gloved hand to me as we went in, smiling suddenly as though he recognized me.

Kaye's was the same inside, the same smells and sizzles of hamburgers on the grill. Even the menu was the same, with some price changes slipped in under the plastic covers. We ordered black-and-whites like we always did, and I wouldn't let myself listen when Kaye asked how we were carrying on and Dad explained quietly that it had been hard since Mrs. Hallett had passed away. As if "passed away" meant anything. I didn't look at Kaye when I knew she was looking at me with sad and soulful eyes, probably like those of the lonesome singer.

"Black-and-whites up!" hollered someone in the kitchen, and I spun around. Beyond the counter where Kaye kept all her silverware, ketchup, maple syrup, and napkins, and through a window cut into the kitchen, Will Hurd was setting glasses under the red lights of the lamps. He was the pastor's son, and so had to sit in the very front pew of Albion Grace Church of the Holy Open Bible every Sunday of his entire life. He held his hand up, just like the kid outside, and then went back into the kitchen.

Kaye lowered the foaming glasses into their metal holders and slid them towards us, pushing the napkin dispenser along after them. "Here, honey," she crooned to me, "best drink up. You'll be just skin and bones if you don't." She brought over a bowl of nuts and set it beside my plate.

Will passed the kitchen window, carrying stacks of plates and sometimes looking my way, probably because he had never seen someone with a dead mother. I decided not to look and drank deeply, the cold so hard against my throat it hurt.

Dad kept talking to Kaye, telling her about his trombone playing, about how we were moving up here to Albion. She listened to him chatter as though she had nothing else in all the world to do. He laughed as though this were any other summer. The black-and-white started to feel real heavy. I let the nuts be.

When we left, the guy outside was still brushing the parasol. And suddenly it was Ma up there, brushing off the top of the beach umbrella, and I was squatting on the sand of a lakeside beach and looking at my mother's hair, which was tied back except for the wisp that came down into her eyes, and she was smiling to show that she was glad to be around me. Then Dad started the car.

I wondered how long I'd been staring at the parasol. I figured I had to say something. "Not a fun job," I called.

"Nope, but it's a job. Right now Will Hurd and I are Dining Constructors, Inc. You visiting?"

"We're moving to Albion."

"At least you say it right." (If you lived in Albion, you used two syllables to name the town. Everyone else in New Hampshire used three.) "Whereabouts you moving in?"

"To my grandparents' place, the Emerson farm."

"Then maybe I'll see you soon. Will and me, we go fishing around there some. Will's the one inside. I'm Peter."

"Cole," I said, touching my chest. "But there's not much good fishing around there."

"Past the top of Cobb's Hill there is. Up by the Great Hosmer. You fish?"

"Yup."

"Then you have to see Will fish. He charms them. He knows when they want to bite, and where they are, and what time of day they're napping."

"How can he tell all that?"

"No one knows. Maybe God. But Will's like that about everything. He can find a doe's nest and tell by its feel how long it's been since she's been there and whether she had one or two fawns. He can tell you when the moon is going to rise, where the lightning will hit, and when the first snow will come. His father says he would have been burned at the stake three hundred years ago."

Dad jabbed at the car horn. "See you," I called, and he gave me a backwards wave before turning back to the parasol.

So we drove out of town, up River Road. Grandpa's farm was about a mile and a half out from town. It had been in the family so long that it didn't need an address. People used to write to him, Hiram Emerson, Albion,

11

New Hampshire, and the letter always came. Sometimes I thought there wasn't much difference between him and the clapboard house that looked over the fields behind, gold with winter wheat, the afternoon wind pushing through it like the breath of God. Or maybe he was more like the gray sheds that connected the house to the weathered red barn: the milk store, the supply room, the farm office, the hay store, the chicken coop, and the back shed filled with furniture waiting to be fixed from two and three generations back. Everything smelled of old wood except the workshop; that smelled of new curls left over from the cedar chests that Grandpa made. Most houses in Albion had one except for his own. Grandma couldn't abide the smell it put into blankets.

Grandpa could hardly talk about the farm without tearing up. There was too much of him in it. Sometimes, right about sunset when the shadows were long and warm, he would stand and watch the fields that stretched all the way to the south pine woods, like his father had before him, and his father before him. Nothing about the land had changed in all that time; it was still the same view. I could imagine all three of them standing there together, looking over these same fields. Sometimes it made me shivery.

I knew the farmhouse was old—not as old as some in Albion, but old. Grandpa still had the deed for the farm, signed by Hieronymous Emerson himself in June 1844. Beyond this deed I knew almost nothing about Hieronymous, except that he was my great-great something or other and he lived in this house all his life. I figured that I would probably never know more than that.

And there, of course, I was wrong.

River Road ran along the water between Great Hosmer Pond and Little Hosmer Pond, but I don't think you could properly call what lay between them a river. The road hunched its way around boulders that seemed to have grown there just to shove a car out of the way. Year after year the trees had thickened along the road, darkening it more and more, so now I couldn't see the river at all. If it were mud season, though, the water would have come right up to the hubcaps.

River Road—at least the paved part—ended at the bottom of Cobb's Hill. From there, the road became dirt and followed rigid stone walls that had run there even before Hieronymous. Rabbit hunters had left gaps in the walls last winter, and some of the stones had rolled across and clunked under the car as we ran over them. "If this were all mud, it would be worth our lives to get up it" said Dad, his hands tight on the steering wheel.

But when we reached the top of the hill and saw the house, I suddenly felt that it was worth my life. Hieronymous had built it keeping in mind the weight of the winter snow and the direction of the spring sun. It was in such a perfect place that I could imagine God himself making the spot for Hieronymous. The hill sloped away from it in front, opening the house to the sky and to a perfect view of the lower valley, now all yellow in the fading light. But around the back of the house the hill curled like a quilt, cutting off the northern wind and setting pines to screen the snow.

We drove into the driveway, our tires kicking up the gravel. And there suddenly was Grandma, pushing through the screen door, the light from the kitchen

13

shining out behind her. And Grandpa catching the door as it swung back. And Grandma hugging us, then standing back and studying us some, seeing what the last year—or two years—had given and done. Then more hugging and some crying. And then, a suitcase in each hand, I climbed the porch steps into the kitchen that smelled of fresh bread and blueberry pies and store-bought cucumbers in vinegar and everything good in the world.

TWO

THE HOUSE OPENED ITSELF UP for us like an apple blossom. Grandma had pretty well settled which rooms we were to take. I'd be upstairs in the braided rug room. (It had belonged to Uncle Law.) And Dad would be downstairs in the room that he and Ma had always had since they were married.

But it didn't turn out that way. Dad took the hired man's room above the kitchen. I'd played up there summers, trying out the stovepipe hat that some Emerson had worn to a ball forever and a year ago. Piles of old *Albion Gazettes* hid the corners, an old treadle sewing machine hunched under a part of the ceiling that had fallen in, and the roses on the wallpaper had faded to a color that roses never were. No one went up there in winter; the one window faced north and the rippled glass didn't even try to keep out the cold. It was dark in the room by three o'clock.

But Dad said it was just right, spent a day and a half cleaning, and moved his suitcase in. My grandmother watched his back with watery eyes; it must have been like looking through the rippled glass.

So I ended up in the room downstairs, with its worn wide boards, its big old cupboard, and the seafaring books collected by my great-grandfather, who never once set foot on a boat that had soaked in saltwater: Sir T. Herbert's *Voyages into Asia and Africa,* Obed Macy's *History of Nantucket,* Rev. Henry T. Cheever's *The Whale and His Captors.* A box of family letters held the books upright. Inside, the letters were ribboned and marked by year. On the very bottom were three from Hieronymous himself, whose grave I could see out my window. If I had looked, I would have found the letters I'd written to Grandma and Grandpa, here bundled and ribboned and put away for someone else to read on a rainy day.

I kept *The House at Pooh Corner* right beside the letters. I read it most every night.

I figured it wasn't going to be easy, living with Grandpa and Grandma. Mostly Grandpa. Ma used to say that he was the most cantankerous man in all of Albion, New Hampshire. If you asked Grandma, she would have said that he was the most cantankerous man in all of Portsmouth County, and she might have been right. He could fuss about anything. If I let out just one cuss— just a damn—he'd be on me like I'd broken all Ten Commandments three and four times over. By the time he was through, I wished I'd gone ahead and coveted my neighbor's oxen or borne false witness or forgotten to honor my mother and my father.

Ma said that she didn't know how Grandma put up with him all these years. But I knew: He loved her more than he loved his eyes. You could see it every time he looked at her. She'd walk into the best room, and he would look at her and start to pray, thanking the good Lord that He had given his cantankerous self this good woman. She knew what he was praying and she'd smile and carry on with her dusting.

All she had to do was touch him and he would come out like dandelions in May. He could be at the front door, laying into some salesman for disturbing his reading Zane Grey, and she'd walk down the stairs, touch his shoulder, and next thing you knew, he was inviting that salesman in out of the cold for coffee and a sugar doughnut, like he was a neighbor or something. That's how they ended up with two vacuum cleaners, a set of the *Encyclopaedia Britannica* complete with yearbooks into the next millennium, and a pile of literature from the Church of Latter-day Saints, which they kept in a box at the foot of the basement stairs.

They kept the whole pile down there because they didn't want to throw out something religious, but neither did they want Pastor Hurd to see it, him being a Baptist and not too keen on other denominations. Maybe Grandpa figured he was enough of a tribulation to Pastor Hurd, without him seeing literature from the Church of Latter-day Saints in the house.

For Grandpa, Sunday services were an opportunity. He liked to sit in the front pew, close up to Pastor Hurd, and take notes all through the sermon on the back of that week's prayer list. When everyone went to shake the minister's hand at the end of the service and tried to say something polite while they were thinking about getting their roasts on, Grandpa handed the list to Pastor Hurd. "Read it when you get a chance," he'd say. Pastor Hurd used to read it on the spot, and his cheeks would flame up at the List of Theological Errors that Grandpa had written.

"Thank you, Hiram," he would whisper. It got so that Pastor Hurd just took the list, put it in the side pocket of his robe, and smiled a smile so tight that his lips would twang if you touched them.

But Grandpa wasn't cantankerous with everyone.

If Pastor Hurd had seen Grandpa with Anne, Emily, and Charlotte, he would have thought he was looking at a different person. Grandpa would never sell those cows, figuring they had stood by him when he needed them, and he would stand by them now. He'd cuddle them on their noses, run his hand along the silky hair on their snouts, and then scratch them up behind the ears like they were dogs. Everyone knows that most cows are mean and all cows are dumb, but these three—they loved him like he was their mother.

And Grandpa still had one horse, The Frisian. He mostly lolled around the back fields, too old to pull, too ornery to ride, but honored for years of work. In his prime his hooves and flanks were so great that he could pull out stumps by himself without breaking into a lather. Now his muzzle was gray and he moved as though he were brittle. But it didn't matter to Grandpa. He kept his feathery legs brushed, his sides curried, and his mane combed out like

17

he was up for show. And maybe, for Grandpa, he was.

Grandpa was like that with everything on the farm. Let anyone tell him his animals were past prime or that his McCormick tractor should be traded in for a John Deere, and you'd hear words come out of him that aren't even in the language. He'd been known to kick a deacon in the shins over this.

Grandma pretty much let him have his way with everything on the farm, except for the grove of Limber Twig apple trees, the perennials in the front and side gardens, and the cemetery plots. The apple trees she planted the summer she was a bride, just come to the house. They gave pretty well, enough for the winter's pies and a couple of runs of cider. But the perennials were her real love. She could lay her hands on the loam of those gardens and the roots would start to quiver like they found the Lord. Peonies and shastas and irises would set up straight, poke their pretty noses out at her, and straighten their leaves for inspection. No one else in the family could do it.

The cemetery she needed help with. All the dead Emersons lay down in the Emerson Burial Yard, southeast of the house, where it was warm and the sun hit first thing in the morning. Come summer—earlier if we were there for Memorial Day—Grandma would put me and Grandpa to sprucing it up. She'd stand just outside the stone wall, shouting directions and pointing at what she wanted done. Sometimes we picked up stones fallen from the wall and set them to rights, but mostly we had to rake up last year's oak leaves that never composted. Then we'd cut the grass and take hand clippers to the weeds that grew up along the stones. It was sweaty work, and Grandpa liked to complain about it. "When I'm under here," he'd fuss, "I won't expect the family to slave over my stone."

"I will," Grandma said, and that ended it.

Once Grandpa came up with some concoction he made from a recipe in a magazine to clean the moss off gravestones, but Grandma wouldn't let him touch the stones with it. "Cantankerous old woman," he said, under his breath, and dumped it all out on the lawn. The next morning, the grass where it touched was brown. Nothing ever grew there again.

I was glad the moss stayed on the stones. It softened them some and made the whole place quieter and stiller, like a green comforter tucked right up to the chins of the stones for a cold night.

I liked to run my fingers in the grooves cut in the stones. Sometimes, in the really old ones, the grooves were so weathered that I could hardly make out the Emerson name, but I knew it was under my fingers. In one corner, though, by themselves, three stones leaned back against the wind. One was so weathered that I couldn't read the name at all, but I could tell from what was left it couldn't possibly be Emerson. The other two stones, close beside each other, were mostly blank, but the marks the snows had left showed that whatever it was, it was the same name on both. Aside from these three, Emerson stones filled the cemetery, facing out to the fields to enjoy the view. Some of them had been enjoying it since before the Civil War; one had just begun to settle in.

On the first morning, I went out to see that one stone when the house was still asleep and the sky just turning a grayish pink. The grass around it was clipped back, the white geraniums fresh and neat, holding their dewy heads high. And suddenly it was two years ago and I was standing in cold sunshine. Grandpa crying—the first time I'd ever seen such a thing. Dad's granite face. Pastor Hurd speaking slow and mournful over a proper slash in the earth—"We cannot know God's ways"—and the thud of that dirt, the *thud, thud, thud* shutting off the hollowness around Ma. A stone with no moss.

And then, from out of the house, the mellow tones of Dad's trombone, notes I hadn't heard in a long time, notes of slow, sad songs that shivered the soul inside me. I hardly knew whether any time had passed at all.

I spent the days finding every familiar place. The kitchen first, where we did most of our living by the old black stove with its round lids and water heater and six chromed doors, shined to their brightest. Behind the stove and partly hidden by the great pipe that went up, a row of brass pots lined by size vied with the chrome in shininess. (Grandma didn't use these much since they took so long to polish.) Three cupboards with Mason-jarred home goods, a tin-fronted pie safe, and a breakfront for the glassware that Emersons had been adding to for generations filled up the kitchen.

It was all Grandma's world, the only thing out of place being the double-barrel that Grandpa kept on a gun rack over the back door. He hadn't used it since he last hunted deer, and that was before I was born. "But you never know when you'll need it," he insisted. So it stayed perched up there, the only thing in the room that gathered dust.

But the most familiar places to explore were all outside. I swept the needles from the tree house Grandpa and I had built in a gargantuan pine up in the south woods. I fished the bend below Great Hosmer Pond where I had never caught anything; so far, I kept the record clean. I climbed Cobb's Hill above the house to where it flattened out some and took the trail that Ma and I had marked years ago, coming out to the open place where I dangled my feet over a precipice that fell so fast I couldn't look down without my stomach tightening up.

Lunches were mostly quiet except for Grandpa. He'd talk about chores to be done, how the milk shed needed shoring up against the snow and Emily's stall needed attending to. The McCormick needed two new spark plugs but he'd sent down to Manchester for these, being that Roy Lanier had gotten so confounded modern that he no longer carried the McCormick brand. (Grandma pointed out that no one in New Hampshire carried the McCormick brand anymore, but Grandpa just sniffed and said he didn't see why not.)

Suppers came after Grandpa had checked on the animals, and he'd report on them right after prayer. Emily and Charlotte were fine; that new udder balm had worked well. It looked like it would take a few days to take the chap off Anne's bag though. And The Frisian was back on his feed after a week or so of feeling poorly. Grandma would cluck her tongue at this; Grandpa put out that all his animals were work animals, but we knew that they were more pets. He had me combing at The Frisian's mane and brushing his feathers, but he did all the currying himself, not trusting me to get it right. The Frisian agreed; he only tolerated me. But when Grandpa opened the stall in the morning, he'd crop up his tail and whinny and nudge into Grandpa's overalls to find the apple that waited for him.

"Hiram, you indulge that horse," Grandma said.

"Nothing of the sort, Livia. He's a workhorse. You don't indulge workhorses."

"That horse hasn't worked since before Cole here was born."

"Depends what you mean by work, Livia. Maybe just being a horse is work enough."

At this foolishness Grandma would shake her head and gather the dishes out to the kitchen.

Dad was silent through meals. He used to like to talk about his music and what he was working on, but now he never spoke of it. And he never asked me what I'd been up to. Somehow there just didn't seem much for him to say with Ma gone. New Hampshire made him smaller.

This summer Grandpa wanted to restore the outhouse around back. "Not to use," he assured Grandma. "It's just that every farm should have an outhouse trim and proper." I remembered it in its trim and proper days, before Grandma got her way and Grandpa put in a bathroom. It was a three-holer, though I could never figure out what galactic emergency would make someone need a three-holer. Old calendars lined the walls, all ripped off to December, and an upturned crate held two or three Sears catalogues, most of their pages ripped off too.

It was a good place to sit and think, private as all get-out, and with a sense of history. You couldn't look at those calendars without thinking of time passing.

The outhouse was built at the edge of a small rise, two short posts in front, two long posts in back against the dropoff. It was Grandpa's fault that it had come to grief. He replaced the cedar shingles of the roof with slate, mostly to impress Albion. Who else has an outhouse with a slate roof?" he asked, and everyone had to admit that he was the only one.

But slate is a lot heavier than shingle, and one spring day in mud season Grandpa was sitting and leafing through the Sears catalogue when he felt the long posts beginning to lean backwards. He set the catalogue down and reached for the door, but when he leaned forward, the outhouse leaned backwards all the more. And the more it leaned back, the more the weight of the slate roof pushed those posts farther into the wet ground.

"Livia," Grandpa bellowed, but Grandma was in the front of the house.

Grandpa decided to risk everything in one dash. He aimed his hand towards the door, leaned forward as far as he could—which wasn't very far—and rushed. But he never had a chance. The posts gave, the outhouse toppled over and shattered, and the slate roof sank out of sight.

What Grandpa was covered with when he came in shouldn't be talked about—and never was when he was around.

"Would you want to put on a slate roof?" asked Grandma innocently when Grandpa announced that he wanted to restore the outhouse this summer.

"Livia, sometimes I think there's a cruel streak in you," he answered.

"Hiram," she said, raising her eyebrows, "it was just a question."

He never did get to the outhouse that summer.

Most afternoons we dug in the garden, it being late in the season and the time when weeds felt free to take over and spin themselves around everything that anyone could eat. We worked at them with hoes and trowels. When I reminded Grandpa that there was a shiny red rototiller down to Roy Lanier's Hardware, he looked at me as if I had cussed. "This land has always been hand-farmed," he growled, "and I'm not going to change that just so that Roy Lanier can sell a shiny red rototiller."

"But even Hieronymous must have used horses to plow," I suggested.

"Who says?" he countered. Grandpa wasn't an easy one to argue with.

So we dug, in the sharp blue days of July, while the sun bronzed my back and the garden grew and the sweat fell off me into the dirt to nourish next spring's seedlings. I fell into a rhythm with the hoe, running down the row and turning up the weeds so that their roots dried in the sun. Soon the hoe came easy to my hands and I went eager to the work.

But for Dad, the garden was a battle. He rammed his hoe in too deep and pulled it up, leaving little craters; he scattered soil into the cabbages and once trimmed down a whole line of turnips by mistake—no loss really. He came from the garden red and mean, like from a fight.

In the late afternoons, after finishing a section of the garden, Grandpa, Dad, and I went into the north woods across Cobb's Hill with the long lumberman's saw and took down dead hardwoods. Grandpa called this wood on the hoof, and while we hiked into the dark cool he told us how he and The Frisian used to drag the trunks down to the farm while the snow was on the ground. "Don't need as much now, since the oil furnace," he said, puffing, "so I don't need any more cold feet, cutting in the snow."

It was good to find the right tree, to decide where to fell it, to set the saw against the old bark and feel the rhythm of the cutting begin, the push and pull that spurted sawdust onto the dark soil. Grandpa knew just how far to let the saw cut in before the wood began to pinch, and how far to go on the other side before the tree began to give, and how far we all had to run to be sure the tree didn't buck back at us as it was coming down.

The great splintering crashes—I'll never forget them. First the very top branches would begin to sway, slowly, waving one last time to the clouds. And then the trunk would lean out at an impossible angle, the branches hanging up in the sky for just a moment, caught on something, until the trunk would drag them slowly down to the soil, drag them with bits of sky still attached until the whole thing crashed into the ground and the branches collapsed into a heap, spitting up a few small twigs that spun around in the air one last time.

Then we set to work. First we cut up the smaller branches, carting them back in wheelbarrows into the woodshed, and stacking them, the smell of the sawdust and sap in our noses. Then we took to the trunk with the lumberman's saw, the teeth rasping back and forth until it was cut in stove-length pieces; these too we brought back in wheelbarrows. In the early evening we split—my favorite job. As the days went on, my arms molded to the swing of the maul, until I felt I could do this all day. If I picked exactly the right spot on the log, and if the swing

25

was just perfect, and if the moon and the stars were in precisely the right orbits, the maul would lay into the wood like it was hardly there, and I could stand back, almost with surprise, looking at perfect white splits of wood at my feet.

But where the wood curled around a knot, there was more work. I'd set the wedge and pound, pound it in until the crack crazed across the top of the log, and the wedge would suddenly jump through and I could pull the two pieces apart, sweat coming down my sides.

When you split wood, you can't think of anything else. I split a lot of wood in those July weeks.

We hardly spoke at all, Dad and I, when we were at this. But our work was like a conversation. In the quiet, we each knew who should set the wedge, who should heft the maul, who should stack the pieces, who was tired and needed a spell. Words dropped away from us like sawdust off the logs, so that when we finished at night, our muscles tight from the saw, we could look at each other and know that the work had been good. And more besides. It was almost enough, until he went on up to the hired man's room and picked up his trombone.

Dad and I drove down Cobb's Hill to Albion on Wednesdays to shop at Nolan's Market and General Goods, Grandma's list in hand. We fumbled through all the aisles two and three times to find what Ma used to be able to find without thinking, as though she knew Nolan's mind and could tell where he would put the mayonnaise and the tomato soup. We came to the checkout counter feeling like we had been swimming too long in deep water. In frustration Dad would always grab something just at

26

the end so that we could leave with a full cart, and Grandma's cabinets began to fill up with pumpkin pie filling (no Emerson ever ate pumpkin pie unless he or she was being polite), artificial oatmeal ("Tastes like a chemical," observed Grandpa), and canister after canister of pink lemonade mix ("Too pink to drink," said Grandma).

Mrs. Nolan smiled sadly at us when we checked out. She would sadly shake her head, and sometimes throw an extra pastry into our sacks, figuring, I suppose, that we would grow thin and waste away.

Then on Sundays Grandma, Grandpa, Dad, and I drove down to Albion Grace Church of the Holy Open Bible, a name so long it took three lines on the sign announcing service times. For the most part this was a Baptist church, and so there was no folderol about the place. But there were just enough old Lutherans and Methodists in the church to make Pastor Hurd loosen up and throw in a hymn by one of the Wesley brothers. He wouldn't go any further than that, though. "Smells and bells!" he'd retort if any of his parishioners suggested anything that sounded too Catholic to him.

The Baptists who built this church knew that life was hard and not to be fooled around with. It was a sturdy kind of church, with thick posts down the center and hewn beams against the whitewashed ceiling to hold it up against the snows. Windows were for light, not colored glass. The pulpit was set right at the end of the center aisle, and nothing fancy was carved into it. The organ pipes were spread across the front by size, the only way to hear them properly. The floors were good, honest maple, without a carpet. And the pews were for sitting,

27

not relaxing, so they were plain oak with straight backs.

Once, it was remembered, Mrs. Dowdle brought one of her fancy sofa pillows to sit on and Pastor Hurd changed his sermon midstream to talk about how sin was comfortable like a cushion that we sat easy on. When Mrs. Dowdle failed to make the connection, a visit from one of the deacons ensured that she did not bring the pillow again. Instead, she lent it to Grandpa, who sat on it for eight months despite sermons and deacons until it gave him prickly heat in the summertime.

That first Sunday we all four drove down to church, I didn't want to go. It was already hot and sticky at nine o'clock in the morning, and the day before I'd just found a new spot—shaded and cool and perfect—to fish the Great Hosmer. I pointed out to Dad that we didn't need to start in to churchgoing first thing, now that we'd come to live in Albion.

Dad ran his finger inside his collar to loosen his tie. "No," he answered, "folks here wouldn't understand. They would think we were being standoffish."

"I bet Hieronymous didn't trek all the way from Cobb's Hill into church."

"Hieronymous didn't have a car," he said, "and besides, this is how your Ma would have wanted it." He went back up to the hired man's room to find a different tie.

When we walked into Albion Grace Church of the Holy Open Bible, the organ was warbling softly and two ushers in black suits guarded the door. They shook our hands, and we followed them both up the center aisle of the sanctuary. With no carpet on the floor, my sneakers squeaked twice with each step. I figured that everyone in church knew I had sneakers on before I'd passed three pews.

The ushers stopped by Mrs. Dowdle, who scooted over for us in a flurry of pocketbook, Bible, and bulletin. Dad sidled in after her, and the rest of us followed.

"I was so sorry to hear about Mrs. Hallett," Mrs. Dowdle whispered to Dad, holding on to his right hand with both of hers.

"It all happened a long time ago now," he whispered back. But sitting in that church where I had sat with Ma for nearly every summer I could remember, it didn't seem so long ago.

The hair on the back of my neck rose with all the church's eyes on me. There was the kid whose sneakers squeaked on the wood floor. There was the kid with the dead mother. It was hard not to be angry with Dad for bringing me here. I could be fishing the Great Hosmer by now, hauling something in. It was hard not to be angry with Dad—and with Ma for not being there.

The organ warbled on, vibrating dramatically during the opening prayer and getting loud for "Leaning on the Everlasting Arms." We all stood up to sing: "What a fellowship, what a joy divine." Dad and I shared a hymnal with Mrs. Dowdle, who sang so loud and so high it didn't much matter if I sang at all. So I didn't. Afterwards Pastor Hurd gave another prayer, longer this time, quoting Scripture to God. And then Kaye got up to sing.

Whenever I thought of Kaye, I thought of her in the pastel uniform she wore behind her lunch counter. I never thought of her in anything but that. Her hair was always teased with sweat, her cheeks flushed with the heat of the kitchen; her hands flashing around like birds

29

clearing dishes and swabbing the counter. But now, now she walked slowly up to the front, turned, and looked at us all like—well, not like we were about to order hash and fries.

Then she began to sing.

Her voice came in quiet at first. There was no organ now, so all I could hear in the church was her song, low and still and shivery. At first I didn't listen to the words. The sounds that came out of her mouth couldn't be coming from the same throat that hollered back hamburger orders. No one moved, and Mrs. Dowdle's hands stilled in her lap. If I looked at her, I was sure she would be crying. I even felt Dad stiffen next to me as Kaye sang.

> *"Let us break bread together on our knees,*
> *Let us break bread together on our knees,*
> *When I fall on my knees,*
> *With my face to the rising sun,*
> *O Lord, have mercy on me."*

Kaye's voice moved up and down through the words, softening them and filling them with a longing so tight that I almost forgot to breathe.

The rest of the service wound its way towards lunch. I stood when I had to stand, closed my eyes at the prayers, squashed into the aisle at the end, and shook hands with Pastor Hurd at the door. (No sign of Will, who knew his own way out of church.) The ushers were still there, like guards, and we pushed past them. Then we were in the car, loosening ties and driving back up Cobb's Hill. I wondered if I would have caught anything that morning or not.

But I had caught Kaye's song, or it caught me. It was

30

never far away from me that next week, and I found myself whistling it in the oddest moments: squashing potato bugs, splitting wood, fishing, as I settled down into the couch to read at night. I found, though, that I never whistled it around Dad.

I once heard him trying it out on his trombone, until he discovered that it wasn't a trombone song. At least, not the kind he was playing now. Dad had taken to practicing alone in the hired man's room, wailing out weird and somber songs, and truth to tell, Grandma and Grandpa and I were glad to be out of the house when he was doing this. The sounds sent creepers up our backs, and we found that we could hardly talk to one another when Dad was on the trombone.

But I would rather have heard the weird trombone melodies than the silence that he began to carry around with him more and more, hefting it up on his back each morning and pulling it down over his eyes, his mouth, his whole self. The folds of it were so thick that even Grandma couldn't part them, though she tried, as we sat together in the evenings.

"It must be stifling up in the hired man's room these nights. Maybe you should think again about moving to one of the downstairs rooms. Or at least to one of the rooms in the front of the house. At night the breezes come in so fresh you need a light blanket even."

"Thank you, no." This from Dad, who was staring long into a book without turning any pages.

"I could at least set up that old broad fan. It would clean up nice," Grandma pressed. "Cole, why don't you go carry it down. It's over the stable, covered in something or other.

31

You'll need the flashlight over the stove." I rose from the chess game I was about to lose to Grandpa.

"No," said Dad, louder this time. "It's fine. Everything's fine." He pulled the hood lower over his face.

"Checkmate," said Grandpa, tired.

So I was surprised towards the end of July, when the garden was starting to take care of itself, the good plants shading out the weeds, that Dad suggested we explore Cobb's Hill. On a morning when the buzzing of the cicadas announced that it was going to be a scorcher, we headed up River Road, away from the Great and Little Hosmers. For a time I thought Dad had something to tell me, he looked so tight, like pieces of him could crack off with the sound of a dead branch, but he said nothing as we walked, and after a while I stopped trying to fill in the failed silences.

River Road ran its dusty way for about two miles on past Grandpa's farm; after that it dwindled down to a path that ran through a deserted orchard, the trees scraggly and overgrown, too mean to give fruit anymore. At the far end of the orchard the path twisted past a stone foundation, the mortar still good but the beams and siding all gone, and then it meandered through a grove of birches, some upstarts bright and green, most old and mossed on three sides. We stepped over blackened trunks rotting sweetly among the ferns. Finally, the path pushed through low wild blueberry thickets until it suddenly opened into a graveyard.

I had never been there before that July morning, but I could tell right away that Dad had. He walked into it like the earth was lurching under his feet; his eyes were half closed. He went ahead, and I knew that he wasn't walking with me anymore.

It was a quiet place, maybe the quietest I'd ever known. The spring moss of the ground gave way beneath my sneakers, so I walked among the graves without a sound. Moss had climbed the backs of the slate stones, softening them, quieting them. Nothing moved.

The graves looked off over a ledge, facing the east—the dawn here being too good to miss, I suppose. But it was dark. A great oak in the middle of the yard had grown so tall and so thick that it threw a deep gloom over the stones. There were no other trees; the shade from the oak had smothered them. On beyond the ledge, pine trees hustled down over granite outcroppings, so if you stood at the farthest grave, looking out towards the bottom of Cobb's Hill, you felt like you could jump down to the pine tops that wound like braids on the mountain.

The stones, like those down by Grandpa's farm, were weathered and stained, but I could still make most of them out.

MARY JULE CARTER
1846–1864
BELOVED WIFE AND MOTHER
THE LORD GIVETH AND THE LORD TAKETH AWAY
BLESSED BE THE NAME OF THE LORD

Beside this stone, another small one.

BABY
MAY 1864

I could guess at the story there.

33

Close to the ridge a group of stones slanted, all alike. Each had crossed rifles and a flag so weathered that I could barely make it out.

DAVID LYLE TOLL	GEORGE STUART THOMAS
BORN 1845	BORN 1839
KILLED AT ANTIETAM	KILLED AT CHICKAMAUGA
SEPTEMBER 17, 1862	SEPTEMBER 20, 1863

These stones were all the same. They all told the same story.

I found Hurds, Cottrells, and Gealys up there. But there wasn't a single Emerson, not one.

Still, all those Hurds and Cottrells and Gealys would have known the Emersons. Dead, they would have had to travel past the Emerson farm to this last place, and I wondered how often Hieronymous had leaned against his hoe, watching as the funeral procession went by.

Dad bent down by Mary Jule Carter's stone and began to yank up weeds. "I suppose it doesn't matter much," he said out loud to the air. "No one comes up here anymore, or remembers."

"Remembers what?"

He looked around sharply, as though surprised to hear me. Then he turned back to the stone, pulled up more weeds. "Your mother and I, we would come up here. Sometimes we came just at dawn, when you were still asleep, Cole." He shook his head, smiling. "It was a show. The last stars would be sinking back into the night, and then—no matter how hard we watched we couldn't tell when it really happened—the sky would turn dark gray, then purple, and then paler and paler until the purple turned into a color so bright it has no name, just a feeling. And all the time the air would be chiming and chiming and chiming and your mother and I would be standing here listening and it was all for us." He paused, then stood, his hand on the gravestone. "God, it was all for us."

I knew I should say something, but I didn't know what. His hand clenched over the stone, his fingers green with the wet weeds, his knuckles white with the crushing strain. He's going to break the stone, I thought. It's going to turn to dust in his hand.

"You know what your mother said, every time she saw the sun over those pines? 'Such a great dawning it will be!' And she could tell you all their stories, Cole." His arm swept across the stones. "Somewhere here there's a drummer boy gone off to find glory in war, until he found that there's no such thing as glory in war. And somewhere there's a farmer, Jedidiah something, who planted perfectly straight furrows for ninety-three years, and the day he died both his plow horses broke through their fence and were never seen again. She could tell you all those stories."

"But now, you can tell them."

He shook his head, and stared down at Mary Jule Carter's grave. "No, I've forgotten most of them. I never thought I'd need to remember, because she would always know. 'They're all the same stories,' she used to say, 'all about how we get turned out of the dark woods toward the bright fields of home.'"

"Home is still bright," I said.

"But the woods are much darker. And I've forgotten all the stories."

We turned back, silently, towards the cold foundation. Above us, hawks watched over the stones as they wheeled about on stretched wings, climbing the air above the cliffy clouds.

After that day, Dad spent more and more time in the hired man's room. The weeds in the garden rows that Grandpa had left for him marshaled their forces and retook the furrows, and I spent some time after supper reclaiming them. Much of the wood for winter still needed splitting, and the back wall of the milk shed needed jacking up and setting. But Dad stayed upstairs, alone, playing his trombone some, but mostly not.

I knew what Ma would have done. She would have gone up to the hired man's room, chiding and fussing. She would have lifted the mouthpiece of the trombone and honked a few hearty honks until they were both laughing. Then they would have gone down to the Little Hosmer and waded deeper and deeper until they fell in and came home with bright water in their hair.

But I couldn't do this. I didn't go up to the hired man's room. And I didn't try to bring Dad down to the Little Hosmer.

But Grandma and Grandpa tried some, as much as they could. I guess Grandma thought that Dad was like one of her shastas: All he needed was the right mix of sun, fresh air, water, and fertilizer. Plenty of fertilizer. She combined these in huge lunches on a picnic table by the road. Grandpa and I carted out hefty tomato casseroles, bulging egg salad sandwiches, vats of pickles, whole fried chickens, slices of homemade wheat bread, with rhubarb jam spreading over the edges, and pitcher after pitcher of

36

fresh lemonade. "I don't know if that old table can hold this much potato salad at one sitting," Grandpa said once.

"Hush, Hiram. You know what this is for."

We all put on weight, except for Dad. He didn't eat much at lunchtime, he assured Grandma. He'd make up for it at supper. Grandma smiled and looked over at her daisies, thriving this year.

Grandpa was sure that all Dad needed was a proper job, none of that music business. He spoke to Roy Lanier about it, and one Sunday afternoon Roy came to the house to offer Dad a place at the hardware store. "Maybe you could even get that rototiller sold!" But Dad said no, he'd take some time to himself. When Roy drove away, Grandpa sent me outside to split kindling. Inside, he hollered something that Pastor Hurd would have raised his eyebrows at, and a couple of doors slammed.

Supper that night was pretty quiet.

THREE

THE GOLDEN DAYS OF AUGUST reached on, and I began to feel that I had always lived by Cobb's Hill, that the time with my mother was long gone, that I had been here and would always be here with a father who hid in the hired man's room and who played the trombone—sometimes—late at night. Time was like a fishing line that gets all caught in the reel, looping back into itself and tangling into knots that are forever. And the days' stories were all knitted in the tangles, so that I could hardly remember one day from another.

Other than Grandpa and Grandma, I would have been alone most of the summer if it hadn't been for Peter and Will. I met them both climbing River Road one rainy Saturday morning, just a couple of weeks after we'd moved to Albion.

"Hey," I called, "where you heading?" I knew it was stupid as soon as I asked. They stood and looked at each other; they were each holding rods and Will had a pack.

"Well," said Will. "It's a rainy morning, just perfect for fishing. Kaye gave us our first day off in about a year. And Peter here bought some new hooks and line this morning. I expect we'll spend some time weeding a garden."

"Well," I said, starting to laugh, "maybe not."

"Maybe not," Peter agreed. "You ever fished the Great Hosmer?"

"All the time."

"Catch anything?"

"Not a thing. I don't think there are any fish down there."

Peter started to laugh now. "You mean they're aren't any fish that want to get caught. Hosmer fish, they're old; they know a lot. Can't just anyone catch them."

"Can you?"

"No, I can't. You got to leave it to Will here. He can catch anything that swims."

"Day like today," said Will, winking, "raining and stuff, the fish can't tell the difference between the sky and the water. They stick themselves up to see what's going on, water being in the air. Then they get too cocky, too sure of themselves. And pretty soon they forget everything they know about hooks and worms."

"And then you catch them?"

"And then we catch them. Go get a pole."

Together we went down the field, the grass high and wet, and into the woods that lined the Great Hosmer. We all three dug up worms. It wasn't hard; it was one of those mornings when the rain had seeped into the ground and the worms had come to the surface all in a rush.

Not ten minutes later Will had three speckled trout. They bit at his line like they wanted to be caught, and I half wondered whether Will could just put his hands into the stream to let the trout wiggle to him like puppies. Together we hollowed out a section of the bank and lined one side with rocks to let the water in. Soon the hollow sparkled with trout, all turning their silver-blue sides against one another and flapping the water with their tails.

"Nothing like the rain to bring fish out," said Will.

"Nothing like," agreed Peter.

Around noon we filleted nine trout. From his pack, Will turned out a frying pan and matches wrapped in aluminum foil. Everything was wet, but somehow it didn't seem all that surprising that Will could get a fire going with pine needles, birch bark, and a handful of thin twigs. Peter shrugged his shoulders and looked at me with raised eyebrows as flames spurted up orange and blue and Will started laying on the thicker branches. "After a while you stop asking questions and just accept it," he said.

"Why don't you get out the butter?" laughed Will. "And there's some dry basil and salt."

"Yes, your Magianship," answered Peter, bowing low.

We sat on our haunches as Will fried the trout, three at a time, and then flipped them to us.

No one who hasn't eaten trout fresh out of the Great Hosmer, fried in butter and salt and dry basil, can ever say that they've lived yet.

Will, Peter, and I fished the Great Hosmer whenever we could, and sometimes I even caught something worth pulling in. Kaye didn't give them much time off, but sometimes on a misty morning, when cold drops were collecting on the yellow parasol, she let them go—"No customers on a day like today anyway"—and they were running down River Road before the sun could come out and spoil things, then hurrying me to the water so that we could catch lunch.

Peter had been right about Will. He knew everything there was to know about the woods, and he could show us things that would never have come out on a sunny day: mushrooms swelling with water, moss turning bright green against dark bark, trout jumping to catch the rain, and, once, a deer nest, still dry and warm.

"How did you know this would be here?" we asked, putting our palms against the soft grasses.

Will shrugged. "You just know the kind of place a doe would like to go."

I sat down and hunched up my legs in the nest that a deer had been in just a few minutes ago. Above, some brambles made a perfect roof, and I almost wished the doe would come back so I could curl against her.

If Will knew everything about the woods, Peter knew everything about Albion. I began to bike down to town

40

after chores and supper to meet them coming out of Kaye's, and Peter toured me around. He knew which was the oldest house in town, which two were haunted, which had a fortune in Union gold buried in its cellar, and which had been a station on the Underground Railroad and still had a secret room. He showed me where John Brown had delivered a speech on the Commons before he'd been run out of town, and where Ethan Allen had received a medal—the same one that hangs in Portsmouth County Courthouse today. He could push aside some blackberry vines and show where the old jail had been and tell how it had burned down the night the town tried to lynch a horse thief, and how in the confusion the horse thief had gotten away, horse and all.

There was hardly anyplace in Albion that Peter didn't have a story to tell. Even of Albion Grace Church of the Holy Open Bible.

Being the pastor's son, Will had a spare key to the church—something his father told him not to let the deacons know about. We went in one evening when the mountains were stretching out their shadows against the town. The light came yellow through the pale glass, streaming up and down the aisles. It made us want to whisper.

Our footsteps sounded off the ceiling as we walked up to the pulpit. Will took us around and showed us the carving inside: The initials of every minister who had preached from that pulpit were etched deep into the dark wood. Will ran his finger inside the WH of his father. Not far below it, someone had gouged out a square.

"What's this from?" I asked.

Peter knew. "One minister wanted his initials carved out. He left the church when they wouldn't bury someone in the church graveyard. He packed up and moved out in one night, but not before doing this. No one ever saw him again."

"Who wouldn't they bury?"

"The Sin Eater."

Maybe it was because the light was so low, or maybe it was because I was all shivery already from being inside a church at dusk, but the words fell like weights in the air.

"A Sin Eater," I breathed out loud.

"And a Gealy to boot," added Will. "Kind of makes you wonder about Peter here, doesn't it?"

"It probably was a Hurd who was minister then," pointed out Peter.

"Probably was," agreed Will, "but we'll never know since the initials are gone."

"So where did they finally bury him?" I asked.

"No one knows," answered Peter.

Will leaned forward and whispered loudly: "He's probably still lying around somewhere, waiting in his coffin, hoping someone will come and cover him up. And while he's waiting, let's go see if there's light enough to run some bases."

And so we did, out on the Commons, until it was too dark to see the ball.

The next Sunday during the sermon I thought of the minister coming in late at night, probably all alone, to gouge out his initials. I thought about him through the long prayer and "Abide with Me," and wondered if

Hieronymous had been one of those to keep the Sin Eater out of the church graveyard. But after church there was something else to think about.

Smack in the middle of tomato canning season, Pastor Hurd came up from Albion to call on us.

I'd been watching Grandma fuss about the tomatoes for the last couple of weeks. In May she planted three kinds—Best Boy, Best Girl, and Beefsteak—just to be sure they'd all come up at different times. That way she'd be able to keep up with the canning. But it had been a hot summer and it hadn't cooled off much at night, so the tomatoes just kept swelling and swelling, and before they had any right to, they started to blush down to their green bottoms—not just the Beefsteaks, but the Best Boys and Best Girls, like they were misbehaving and ashamed. Soon all fifty-six plants were blushing through the green, eight or nine bulging tomatoes on every plant, hanging heavy against the stakes.

Grandma went out every morning when they were still soaked with dew to check on them; then she'd head into the basement to collect a new batch of Mason jars and start to clean them out. By the end of July there were ten dozen quart jars gleaming in the pantry, in the cupboards, in the linen closet, and along every windowsill, where they prismed the sunlight into rainbows that glimmered on her back while she washed the dishes.

When she saw the first tomatoes were turning gold she went in to Roy Lanier's Hardware to buy another boiler. When she saw that they were all turning gold together she exchanged it for a larger one. Then she went back and bought the smaller one again in case she needed it too.

"Planning on doing some canning this year?" Roy Lanier asked.

"What else would I be buying these for?" Grandma answered, a bit testy.

One morning, after a night when it had been so hot that there was almost no dew, she went out to the garden and found that all the bulging tomatoes on all fifty-six plants, every single one, had rushed to deep red. They were barely hanging on their drooping branches, so full of juice and seeds and pulp they looked about to pop their skins.

She walked back into the kitchen where Grandpa and I were having breakfast. "Lordy," she said. When we looked up at her, she looked back at us with desperate eyes. "Lordy."

Because today was Sunday.

Now, Albion Grace Church of the Holy Open Bible was strictly Sabbatarian. You could go to church in the morning, come back and set awhile as the dinner got put on, eat, and then wash up. But that was about it. I never saw Will on a Sunday. In the afternoons he was allowed to read, play hymns on the piano (though he could add a bass to those hymns that made them sound something different than the way Miss Bradshaw played them in church), and go for a walk back of his house. But that was about all. At night there were evening services, then quiet reading, a Red Sox game during the season, and bed.

But here was Grandma, fresh in from fifty-six tomato plants, all ripe, all about to drop their tomatoes into the dirt, where they would rot in the heat and the wet. "Lordy," she said a third time, her hand reaching back into

44

her hair and her eyes fixed on the ten dozen quart jars.

That morning we sat in church and Grandma fidgeted. She sang faster and louder than anyone else to help Miss Bradshaw pick up the pace. She passed the collection plate along like it was a hot potato, glaring at the slow-stepping ushers who carried it solemnly up the aisles. She thumped her Bible closed at noon to let Pastor Hurd know that it was time to be finishing up. And when the last "Amen" of "Be Thou My Vision" sounded, she hustled me and Grandpa holding his List of Theological Errors out the back door like a mother quail rushing along her chicks.

"Lunch is fend for yourself," she called, running up the back stairs when we got home. Grandpa glared at her retreating back, holding a speeding ticket in his hand.

I hadn't even finished spreading the mayonnaise on my sandwich before Grandma came back from the shed with two bushel baskets.

"This is Sunday!" said Grandpa.

"You remember the year we had that early frost coming up, Hiram Emerson, and how you were out on that tractor before and after church?"

Silence.

"There are fifty-six tomato plants out there. Fifty-six. And they've seen fit to ripen at the same time. On a Sunday. And in ten minutes I want to have a batch of them in here boiling off their skins." She handed us the bushel baskets and went to the sink to fill her three boilers. "You can eat between batches."

"And Sunday prayers?"

Grandma hesitated at that. Grandpa's Sunday prayers were long. He talked to God like one farmer to another, telling Him what needed to get done that week. Still and all it was Sunday. "The short version rather than the authorized," Grandma said, sitting down. And to his credit, Grandpa tried to oblige.

Grandpa and I, still in our Sunday clothes and with sandwiches in our hands, went out to pick. The tomatoes fell off the plants into our hands. Before the ten minutes were up, we were lugging in the first bushel baskets and setting the tomatoes out on the kitchen table, along the counter, in the dishpan, and finally on newspaper that Grandma spread over the floor. And she was grabbing them, dipping them in boiling water, plucking the skins off, and throwing them in a five-quart pot like her life depended on it. Meanwhile the quart jars were boiling and the steam was thickening on the kitchen ceiling and Grandpa, with the ticket sticking out of his shirt pocket, was getting almost as red as a tomato himself.

By three o'clock all the tomatoes were picked and lay in great heaps on the kitchen floor. Grandpa was in the best room, reading the Saturday paper again, Sunday's having been scattered on the kitchen floor. The phonograph was playing hymns, loud. I was cutting off the tomato tops and throwing them in the compost bucket.

And Grandma, Grandma at seventy-four years old, sweat pouring off her forehead, the steam coming up all around her, Grandma never slowed. She'd finished twenty-seven quart jars now and the three boilers had just taken in the new batch of peeled tomatoes. They simmered and started to boil just as Grandma lowered the next batch of Mason jars to sterilize in another pot. And then we heard the front doorbell ring. We heard the phonograph shut off. Heard Grandpa open the front door. Heard "Hello," the voice of Pastor Hurd.

I had to admire Grandma. She didn't panic. She clapped lids on the vats of stewing tomatoes to keep the scent down, whipped off her apron, and rushed up the back stairs. "Make some lemonade," she yelled in a whisper as she disappeared.

By the time I got the lemonade and tray of glasses into the living room, Grandma was there, her face dry and powdered, looking like she'd just been reading through the book of Philippians and waiting for Pastor Hurd all afternoon. She served the lemonade like it was high tea at Buckingham Palace, and if it hadn't been for the sweat collected on the back of her hands, you never would have known that she had been hefting vats of stewed tomatoes across the kitchen.

Pastor Hurd suggested that the weather had been very hot this summer, though not like in '64, when they'd had such a hot summer that all the tomatoes came due on the very same day.

"On the very same day!" marveled Grandma.

"Never known that to happen," Grandpa observed. "Must've been on a—"

Here he was cut short by Grandma's lemonade, which had spilled across his shirt. He thought that he had better go take care of this, and Grandma agreed.

Silence.

And then the stewed tomatoes began to *ping, ping* against the lid of the boilers.

I suppose if I had thought quickly enough I could have said something to cover the sound of the pinging tomatoes, but I was stunned into listening. We all were. Even when Grandpa came back, he simply settled into his chair and looked up at the ceiling, as though the *ping, ping* were coming from on high.

Grandma tried to cover it with the sound of her rocker.

But the pinging got so loud that people in downtown Albion were probably standing on the streets, looking to the sky to see if it was hailing. Grandma rocked more and more quickly. Grandpa was grinning, looking like a loon, and no warning expression on Grandma's face could wipe it off. And the reverend showed no signs of leaving.

I suggested more lemonade.

Grandma offered to help. No, I thought I'd be fine. No, she would be pleased to help. We hustled out together.

Now, Grandma had hands that could stand any heat. She could take pies out of the oven without mitts, and I've seen her lift lobster pots boiling away right out of coals on the beach. But these pots had been boiling for some time now, and their bottoms were glowing red. She hefted the first, jerking it off the burner, and almost got it to the kitchen counter.

The crash, the swooshing of boiling stewed tomatoes across the linoleum, the vibrating ring of the lid were all heard out in the living room. "Is everything all right?" Pastor Hurd called.

A strangled "perfectly" floated back into the living room. Meanwhile the sea of stewed tomatoes reached to new shores, wave after wave flowing under the door to the basement and down the stairs, behind the woodstove, under the kitchen table, up to the molding, bubbling and boiling and sticking seeds everywhere. I took the lemonade to the living room, careful to leave my sneakers behind when I left the kitchen.

At church that night, Pastor Hurd preached on the Hebrew children gathering up manna each morning and using it during the day. "And on the sixth day, they gathered enough for two days. And all those who gathered more than they needed found that the manna had turned as rancid as—" here there was a long pause, long enough for him to find Grandma's eye—"as rancid as spoiled tomatoes." On the way out, Grandpa took the slip of paper from his shirt pocket—he'd made only a short list, his mind being elsewhere—and handed it to Pastor Hurd. Later, at home, Pastor and Mrs. Hurd tried to figure out why Hiram Emerson had handed him a speeding ticket.

Grandma left church walking kind of stiff. She'd spent a couple of hours on the linoleum, getting the tomatoes up before they stained and hardened. Grandpa had watched from the kitchen door, pointing at likely places for seepage and wondering if he'd be able to find the Sports section of the Sunday paper and read it through the juice.

When Grandma finished, she stuffed all the rest of the tomatoes in plastic bags and chucked them in the freezer. "They'll have to do for spaghetti sauce," she said.

"That's a whole lot of spaghetti sauce," Grandpa suggested.

Grandma said nothing and carted the rest of the Mason jars downstairs until peaches would come in.

Just after dawn on Monday, Grandma was in the Emerson Burial Yard with a bristle brush in hand, scraping at the stones like she was paying some sort of penance for working on the Sabbath. I dressed to the rhythm of

49

the scritches of the brush, and before she was done with old Hieronymous's stone I was with her, pruning away the grass that had grown up almost to the dates on the stones. With the new sun on their backs and the scratching of the bristles, the stones seemed to stretch out like The Frisian, eager to feel the strokes.

Grandma was going at the stones something fierce, but calmed down some when I came and started in on the second generation. We did not speak. It was the kind of time when two people are doing something that pleases them, and they're glad to be doing it with each other, and there's no need to wreck the silence. There was pleasure in trimming the grass right down to the feet of the stones, uncovering a line of a poem that the weeds had hidden, digging out the dirt from a weathered letter with a fingernail. In the sunlight it didn't seem that there could ever have been any real unhappiness here, just a kind of stillness—the kind you find sometimes in an empty church.

But there was sadness too, a sadness sweet and hard in the memory. I watched Grandma brush the small stone of Helena Emerson, her daughter, who had only three days of air and light. Her hand paused and she mouthed the inscription: "God has taken Helena, for His own sweet bud." And then she went on to the next stone, her other daughter, Ma. We trimmed around that stone together, and Grandma plucked the dead blossoms off the white geraniums.

We spent much of the morning in the burial yard. I stopped to run in for breakfast, and we both paused to wave to Grandpa, *put-puttering* off in the McCormick to check on the Christmas trees he'd planted last fall. But otherwise we kept at it as the sun started laying hot hands on our backs and the water Grandma had brought out warmed.

She started in on the two blank graves while I trimmed the stone with no name. "You sure we need to do these as well?" I asked.

"May as well finish a job that's started."

"They're not Emersons."

"No," she said, "but we owe it to them."

"Owe it to them?"

Grandma stood up, bristle brush in hand, looking suddenly puzzled at the three stones. "You know, now that you ask, I'm not sure why we owe it to them. It's what Hiram's father used to say, and I suppose his father said it before him. And now Hiram says it. But I don't know why these three are buried here."

"Maybe these are related to the Emersons."

"If they are I don't know how." She began to rake dead leaves from the bottom of the stones with her hands. "I guess somehow they wandered up here."

Back to the house, the screen door slammed and Dad walked out, mostly hidden by the shadows of the maples that grew outside the pantry window. His hands were deep in his pockets and pulled his shoulders down. He looked up at us, and then at Ma's stone. For a moment he seemed to be about to come over, but he hunched away behind the house up towards the pine woods. Grandma looked after him a long time.

"It's not hard," she said out loud, but not really to me, "to wander away from where you're supposed to be."

I finished trimming the grass from in front of the stone

with no name and went around back, where a thatch of grass had grown high and thick. I curled it away from the stone with my fingers, scraping my knuckles against the granite and scenting the sweet mint mixed in the grass. If the light hadn't been just so, and if the stone hadn't been wet with dew, and if the dirt hadn't forced its way into the letters, I wouldn't have seen that words had been carved into the stone—on its back. The thatch had protected them from weather, and they stood out now, as sharply cut as they must have been when they were first chiseled in: WHO ARE WE TO JUDGE? I had to lie on my stomach to see them, and by the time I had gotten up, Grandma had left the burial yard and wandered out a little ways towards the field, where she watched Dad slowly make his way up to the pines.

I trimmed the thatch away and let the words dry in the sun.

After last night's sermon, Grandma had decided not to profit from her breaking of the Sabbath, so that afternoon, Grandma and I brought every jar of stewed tomatoes over to Mrs. Dowdle, who loved stewed tomatoes but whose knees prevented her from growing them anymore. She had thick legs and thick arms and wore black dresses with cut rubies like she was always ready for a funeral. But she had a high, horsey laugh that came out suddenly to let you know that she wasn't thinking much on funerals.

Miss Cottrell had come from her house on the square and was visiting over tea. Miss Cottrell visited properly. She called days in advance to set up a punctual time. When she appeared, she came bedecked in pearls and rings and a touch of rouge on each cheek. Her shoes were square-heeled and square-toed because she would have none of this world's fancy fashions. Because she knew everyone in Albion and had known them since they were born, she felt that she could talk about them all freely, and I always had the uncomfortable feeling that she knew things about me that I wasn't so sure of myself.

In Mrs. Dowdle's best room, Grandma was quiet, holding her thin teacup, but it didn't matter much since Miss Cottrell had enough to say for just about everyone. I hadn't seen her in two years, of course, and she talked about me like she had for every summer I could remember.

"You've grown so much," she said, cupping my face between her two powdery hands. "Just look at you, so much like your mother at this age, with the Emerson cheekbones and nose, and my, just look at those Emerson ears—the same as Hiram had—and I bet you're smart as a whip just like him and just like his father—God rest his soul—the smart-alecky one in our school and I bet you're just the same, probably have every girl just swooning over you too . . ."

Miss Cottrell could talk without periods.

Grandma and Mrs. Dowdle went into the kitchen to put away the tomatoes, and Miss Cottrell followed them to give advice on how they should be stored. "You need a cool place but one that's handy so that you can reach them—so pretty they are—no, that won't do there, but Olivia, I wonder that you find the time to put these up when you have a young boy to feed now . . ." Her voice trailed off.

Mrs. Dowdle's best room was filled with all the clutter of a 150-year-old house that had been lived in by the same family for generation after generation. In the early morning on a bright day, a beam of sunlight toured across the room, first striking the family tintypes that were stuck to the walls like memories. Around noontime the beam lit on glass pitchers and thin teacups and flow-blue plates tilted just so in their glazed cabinets, as ready for a tea party now as they had been at the end of the last century. By early afternoon the sunbeam slanted low through the leaded panes and settled easy on the quilted chairs; they were old friends and faded into one another. One errant beam would glance off the marble-topped table in the room's center and scatter gleaming onto the rounded glass covering the bookcases, to shine onto faded spines and yellowed pages.

I sat on a flowered sofa beneath the tintypes, sitting as still as people in those pictures, who posed stiffly so they wouldn't blur; I could almost hear the photographer underneath his black cloth, warning them to hold still. Some were solemn wedding pictures, some posed baby shots (all blurred in the face), and one a funeral gathering, everyone standing around an open casket, no one looking in. Across the bottom of a street scene the photographer had scripted *Main Street, Albion, New Hampshire, 1871,* but none of the buildings that stood then stood now. Brick had replaced clapboard, and the dirt road had been covered over with asphalt. Blurs walked on the wooden sidewalks, and the only thing that was the same was the range of mountains off in the distance. It seemed like there should have been some sort of moral in that.

All this I had seen before; a visit to Mrs. Dowdle's was part of our normal summer routine. Ma had dressed Dad and me up as though it was a Sunday, turned a deaf ear to our fussing, and herded us over to Mrs. Dowdle's best room to suffer an afternoon of dried lady fingers and warm tea with milk. ("It's not good to drink anything too hot or too cold.") Sitting there listening to stories about people who had died before my parents were born was like sitting in a stadium during a rain delay: You know that it's going to end sooner or later and then you'll get in your car and go home.

Afternoons at Mrs. Dowdle's were long, long rain delays.

But this time, while Miss Cottrell was settling on the right place for the stewed tomatoes, I saw something new. Well, not new. It was a tintype as old as all the rest, but hanging lower and in the shadow of the bookcase, as though it didn't want to be seen. A man leaned against a pine; the wide brim of his hat hung low over his forehead. But even with the hat he held his hand up to shield his face, perhaps from the flash of powder. His clothes were patched, and his arms came out a long ways from his shirtsleeves, but you could see that he wasn't interested in apologizing for it. In fact, the more I looked at him, the more I knew that he was—it's hard to find a word for this—content. Not happy, but content. And I can't tell you why he looked that way. Maybe the air just seemed to rest easy on him.

Mrs. Dowdle came out to fetch me into the kitchen. "Young Cole," she said, "we've found just the place but we need you to bring up the stepladder from the basement."

"Mrs. Dowdle, who is this?" I asked, pointing to the tintype.

She came over and peered into the shadows. "The Sin Eater," she said simply. "He was a Gealy. Now come along. Your grandmother's waiting."

The rest of the visit was spent bringing jars to their places as Miss Cottrell fussed about their being too high up. But while I pushed the jars back into the cupboard, the face of the content Sin Eater hovered in front of me like a sunlit ghost.

FOUR

THE DOG DAYS OF AUGUST hobbled in as though on three legs, leashed back by morning storms through most of the beginning of the month. But once they came, they settled in with a vengeance, as Grandma said. The sun withered down until everything hung limp—the sheets on the back line, the cornstalks, the hard green leaves on the front lilacs, and especially Dad, who seemed to leach away into the ground.

It only took about two or three days to dry the fields, and as soon as we could walk across the haymow without squelching up water, Grandpa honed the shears on the mower and carted it out into the sun. Years ago he'd pulled it with The Frisian. But now Grandpa hauled the mower with the McCormick, coughing some on the diesel combustion. He called to the tractor as he had called to The Frisian: "Haw! Haw! Haw! Git up, now! Git up!"

The McCormick didn't listen, but then neither had The Frisian, so Grandpa had no real point of comparison. The Frisian seemed to realize this as he lumbered along behind the mower, tossing his head in the sun and flattening the hay with his great hooves.

Three times a year for seventy-four years this mower had cut a field, and for each one there was a notch nicked into its crossbeam. Grandpa let me notch the beam this time with his Buck knife, and then motioned for me to climb up with him. He kept his face looking away.

For two days, under skies as white as old ice, Grandpa, I, and The Frisian mowed the back fields, the second mowing of the year—late because it'd been so wet. The *clack-clack-clacking* of the mower, the rattle of the cutting bar, the swooshing of the grass under the scything, the smooth oiled growling of the engine were so loud we couldn't talk, but there was no need to. We stopped at midday when Grandma stood at the edge of the field with fresh-squeezed lemonade and a basket, and while The Frisian stalked back to his trough we ate a packed lunch together under the three oaks centering the field. And then back to mowing until the sun was high and it was too hot to do any more. The stubble in the field broke sharp beneath our boots as we walked back home over it.

On the third day, we raked the hay into long rows that spiraled around the field, and on the fourth, we turned it all over to dry in the August sun. On the fifth, Henry Cooper came from his farm with his new John Deere tractor and his baler. After a decade of repairs, our baler had given up the ghost and Grandpa had asked Mr. Cooper to help out. He was happy to oblige, mostly because he loved to ride on his John Deere, especially this new one. It was one of those tractors that looked alive, like it had strength seething under its green skin. Even Grandpa was impressed by it, but he'd never admit that to Mr. Cooper, who was, truth be told, a little afraid of Grandpa.

Mr. Cooper raced around the field, power in his hands, the baler's long spidery arm jerking webs around the bales and scooting them out, scattering rectangles of hay across the field all helter-skelter. Grandpa and I stood at the edge of the field with The Frisian and watched. Mr. Cooper finished before he had any right to.

"That's it, Mr. Emerson," he called from his perch on the John Deere. "This machine makes short work of most any job."

"Seems so," growled Grandpa.

"You need me to come and collect these tomorrow?"

"No thanks, Henry. You've done enough. Cole and I will handle the hauling."

Mr. Cooper shrugged his shoulders, settled back into his seat, and with a smooth and satisfied roar set his back wheels turning. He seemed so high up that he must have been able to look in the second-story windows of the house as he passed, and driving down River Road he waved jauntily at any car that drove by.

On the sixth day, Grandpa and I put on thick leather gloves and long-sleeved flannel shirts. Broiling under the sun, we hefted the bales high and higher onto the trailer that Grandma drove slowly alongside us, her back straight on the McCormick. Afterwards we carted the bales into the barn, afraid to look at them lest a glance topple the load. The gold dust was heavy in our nostrils and the hay sweet as sugar.

When I settled the last bale onto the very top, leaning down with my back scraping the barn roof, I saw Grandpa reach up and pick out the bits of straw stuck in Grandma's hair. They walked back to the house ahead of me, and I biked into Albion to find Will and Peter, who by this time would just be finishing up at Kaye's.

During the wet days, we'd fished the Great Hosmer most every afternoon, and even though the trout didn't jump up to me like they did for Will, at least they were friendly enough to let me reel them in once in a while. I even got to where I could throw my line out halfway across without catching it on an overhanging maple, or across Will's line, or, once, on Peter. (That riled him some.)

But after mowing, when you're covered with hay dust, it isn't fishing you're aching for, it's swimming. Will knew a place below Albion where the Little Hosmer ran out cool and fast into two pools, one waterfalling into the next. Granite ledges surrounded each pool, fifteen feet above the first, but right even with the water on the second. Hardly anyone went there, he said, because it was so hard to get to. And it was. A two-mile ride down Route 23 on burning asphalt, a rutted path that got thinner and muddier the farther we went, trees that sprawled out their roots to trip us up, and finally a trail too thin to bike on, covered with thin shale flaked off into sharp arrowheads.

But once we got there, I knew it was worth it. We stripped by the ledges, and when we stood on top, I felt the cold of the water pushing up against us, and its roar and rush churned in my stomach. If Will felt it, it didn't make him wait a second. He dove down, so straight and perfect, so easy that he and the waterfall seemed to dive into the pool together. Peter and I watched as Will's head popped out of the foam and he turned on his back to let himself be carried to the green, still water at the pool's side. Will hollered, but we couldn't hear him over the sound of the falls.

Peter jumped next, his hand squelching his nose closed. I curled my toes around the edge of the ledges, forced down the fear that gutted my stomach, and dove. I felt myself moving with the waterfall, the foam all around me, and then I was in the pool, so cold that the chill gripped my bones. The force of the falls pushed me up and out, and I let myself float in the cold underwater, where there was no sound but the muted roar of the waterfall, where everything moved slowly, where everything was so simple. I just let myself be pushed along; I didn't have to do anything. And then I was at the surface.

Will and Peter stood at the edge of the pool, their feet in the water, knees bent to steady themselves against sliding on the moss. "You sure took a long time to come up."

"Let's go again," I said.

For the rest of that afternoon, until the pine tops started to prick the edge of the sun, we dove into the pool, clambered up the ledges, and dove again. The shock of the cold was startling every time, and I wondered if my whole body would be numbed. But it never was and we dove on and on.

Sometimes we dove together and then raced to the side. Sometimes we dove and tried to see how far we could let the water push us. Sometimes Will somersaulted into the cascade. (This is something Peter tried, coming up with water in his nose.) And sometimes we all came up quickly and floated, faces to the perfect glass dome above us and the pines waving their tips to the clouds, until we bumped gently against the shore.

When the sunlight yellowed we climbed to the top of the ledges to let the air dry us.

"What a great place," I said. "I've never swum in a place like it before."

"It's perfect," agreed Will, leaning back and spreading his arms behind his head. "Just perfect."

I lay back too, contented. If there was a place away from all the world, this was it. Suddenly I imagined Dad up here, out of the hired man's room. I smiled, almost laughed at the thought. I could see Dad trekking along the path, climbing the ledges, and then diving into the waterfall. I could just as well imagine him sprouting six wings and lofting to the moon.

When suppertime started to edge up on us, we dressed and began the long climb back. It was the first of many afternoons together at the ledges.

The night the haying was over, Grandma always baked early green apple pies, cinammon and sugar clumped on top. Midsummer all she had left were last fall's punky apples, good for applesauce but not pies. So in mid-August she went out eagerly to collect a few early greens from the Limber Twig apple trees, picking them with a careful hand. With cold milk and vanilla ice cream melting on the side, Grandma's early green apple pies were the kind of dessert you could think about all day and never be disappointed in when it finally came.

"You know, Cole," Grandpa said that night, "I believe this pie is just about as good as the one that lost out to Miss Cottrell at the fair six years ago."

Grandma gave him a cold eye. "I did not lose out to her pie."

"I remember that you did."

"Then you don't remember very well. What happened was that she used the recipe that's been in our family ever since Erastus Emerson planted green apple trees at the bottom of the front field. Then she sat there and said it had been in her family for a hundred years. I never heard such a bald-faced lie, and Mrs. Hurd standing right behind her."

"Well," said Grandpa, pushing back from the table, "whether Cottrell or Emerson, this one is a fine recipe. Eh, Cole?"

"It's Emerson," said Grandma, turning to the kitchen.

I gathered up some of the dishes. Grandpa headed to the back door, then paused with it halfway open.

"Say, Cole, after you've gathered those you want to come out and help me clean up the mower?"

"Sure."

"After a couple of nights the grass starts to stick to it, and we don't want to have to clean it tomorrow, it being Sunday and all. Right, Livia?"

Grandma dropped a whole pile of dishes into the sink and turned the water on full blast.

Towards the end of August things slowed down at Kaye's Cafe and she let Will and Peter have Saturdays off, raining or not. The very first one they had free we decided to camp out above the ledges. At the last minute, though, Peter had to go down to Keene to his cousin's confirmation service, and his folks didn't listen when he told them he didn't care whether his cousin was confirmed or not. They passed us heading south on Route 23, Peter pulling his bow tie away from his neck so it wouldn't crush his Adam's apple, us biking with two full backpacks, holding up the bottoms of the packs with our left hands so they wouldn't scrape against the wheels.

Grandma and Mrs. Hurd must have thought we'd be gone for a week or so; Will said that we had just about enough food to feed the five thousand. Canned beans, sliced cucumbers, four cans of soup, celery and carrots, half a dozen peanut butter and honey sandwiches, eggs and sliced bacon, fruit cookies, four oranges, two boxes of raisins (large size), a package of twelve frankfurters and twelve buns, and a bag of marshmallows—we ate it all except for three franks that fell into the fire and sizzled into ash. We saved the bacon and eggs for breakfast.

After dinner and a swim, we collected wood until it was too dark to see beyond the fire. We sat, whittled, and told ghost stories. I could never get these right. When Dad told me about the guy with no face, screaming with no mouth and blundering about the forest, I'd hunched into myself like a cocoon. But when I told it to Will, he just laughed.

"Sorry, Cole, sorry. It really is a good story."

"Yeah."

"It really is good, Cole. I'm not laughing at the story."

"So what are you laughing at?"

A pause.

"Well, I guess I am laughing at the story."

I threw a piece of kindling at him. "So let's hear yours."

"Okay. And you can't laugh at this because it's true."

"Uh-huh."

"It is. About a mile up this water there's the farm of the Sin Eater."

I don't know if it was the name or one of the stones cracking suddenly in the fire that startled me. But after that, everything in the world stilled except for Will's voice, and it seemed as if he wasn't telling a ghost story as much as telling a secret.

"He lived up here all alone, and never came into town but once or twice a year to buy a kettle, or shells, or a knife. No one talked to him, and no one ever touched him, because he could eat sin. He could grab it in his two hands and roll it tight. Then he'd pound it into bread dough and work it in good. And then he'd bake the sin until it rose and got hot and then he'd eat it down."

"Where did he get the sin?"

"Anybody who'd give it to him. And when he couldn't get enough, he'd go sin himself—cuss or steal a pig or murder someone, probably. Anyway, his farm was on rocky ground and people before him hadn't been able to grow near enough there to keep them. But the Sin Eater, he could grow any crop you could name. His corn grew so fast that he could put in two plantings, one for June, one for August. His pumpkins were as big as barrels, and apples the size of your head. Folks around here knew that he'd made a pact with the devil to grow like that, so they wouldn't buy from him and he'd have to sell down in Boston."

"You can't make a pact with the devil."

"You can if you've stuffed yourself with sin until you're ready to burst. And that's how the Sin Eater was. He'd wander down to Albion at night, stick his head in somebody's window, and catch the sins that people remember in their dreams. He probably stuck his head in the window of your very own bedroom back then, Cole. And then he'd carry all those sins to his place, bake them into a loaf of bread, and eat them up.

"Year after year he ate sin, and year after year it grew in him, not so that you'd see it, but you could tell by his eyes. They'd glow at night, so that he had to keep them half closed while he prowled about town.

"One night there was a thunderstorm, so bad that folks said it was the devil himself come to visit his good friend. When they met, the sin was so hot that it burned half the mountain, and the next day nothing was left of his farm but the stone foundation and chimney. Everything else was burned clean to the ground. They found his body, all charred, and they went to town to get a coffin. But when they came back, the body was gone. Some said there was so much sin in him that he couldn't die and his body just got up and walked away. And some said that the devil carried him off. But there was nothing more they could do up there, so they went back down and let the farm smolder.

"Albion would have forgotten all about the Sin Eater except for one thing. A week later there was another lightning storm, almost as bad as the first. And when folks looked out through their windows at the storm, they saw glowing eyes looking at them, and heard a thin, high voice, calling for their sins."

I didn't laugh. "A true story?"

"Mostly. It's what some people still say."

We settled into our sleeping bags, me with my hands behind my head, looking through the branches like nets catching at the stars, thinking about what people said. "Will, there really was a Sin Eater, you know."

"I know. I just told you."

"I wonder how he got the name."

"That's what he was. A Sin Eater."

"You can't eat sin. It's not something you can lay your hands on and stuff into bread."

Will thought for a bit. "But suppose you believed that you could? Suppose you really believed that you could take someone else's sin and eat it? And suppose people believed that you could do it?"

"But why would you do it? It doesn't make sense. Even if you could, why fill yourself with someone else's sin?"

"Maybe," said Will slowly, "because the Sin Eater didn't really go out to look for it. Maybe because people gave it to him, and he wanted to hold it for them."

"Hold it so that he could live," I said.

"Or so that they could die," Will answered. He got up and banked the fire, and I fell asleep watching the sparks head up into the night sky, yearning to be stars.

The morning came cold and fuzzy, the sunlight white against the trees, our sleeping bags wet with the dew, a single wisp of smoke escaping slowly from the firepit. I dusted the ashes off the embers, added some birch, and got the fire crackling again. Will took the sleeping bags out to the ledges to let the sun dry them. He fried bacon and cooked eggs in the grease—there is nothing like eggs and bacon over a fire outside—and after we ate we scattered the wood and doused the fire, the water hissing against the hot rocks, and headed upstream. Without saying it, we both knew where we were headed: to the Sin Eater's farmhouse.

I'm not sure what I expected to find there, probably the timbers of the farmhouse still black against the green fields, still smoldering. But of course it was all overgrown, and if Will hadn't shown me where to look I might not have seen the chimney sticking up, the bricks covered with vines so thick you couldn't get at them to touch. I could just make out the outline of the foundation, the stones still mortared together. We stepped over and kicked at the dirt with our heels, but it was hard as cement. Almost nothing left of a life lived there.

But we weren't saddened by it. On one side the creek bubbled along on its way to the ledges like it had been doing for who knows how long. On the other the fields stretched out to the low hills, where they climbed and rushed to hide themselves in old woods. The cicadas were singing and bees bumbling around masses of purple asters that had grown up around the south side of the foundation. Though the house was gone, everything was as it had been for a very long time.

We got back home late, when the sun was starting to slant the shadows. Grandma had fixed a supper that was more than any human could eat, but she figured I probably hadn't eaten right all day. Dad fixed a plate and took it up to the hired man's room—he said he didn't feel well—but Grandpa and Grandma and I sat down to chicken fried crisp, potato salad topped with hard-boiled eggs, cucumber slices, pole beans, and thick wedges of homemade bread with raspberry jam. It was one of those meals where you get full about halfway through, but you keep eating because you know that someday you'd regret not tasting that potato salad or chicken leg. And by dessert time you're eating to be polite, until you realize that somehow your life wouldn't be complete if you didn't eat that slice of wild blueberry pie.

"You go up to the ledges again, Cole?" asked Grandpa.

"Yeah," I said, pushing my chair back and stretching out my legs. "And then up a ways to the Sin Eater's farm."

I wondered if they would know about the farm, and they did.

"You remember those asters you picked up there for me, Hiram?"

He did.

"And the picnic we had on the stones of that place?"

He remembered that too. They looked at each other a long time, like they were remembering a day that was so perfect they didn't want to share it with anyone else, because sharing it would be giving part of it away.

"You think there really was a Sin Eater?" I asked.

"Sure there was," said Grandpa, chewing the crust of the pie. He always saved this bit for last, and he would run it around the blueberry juice.

"Hurry up, Hiram. I've got these dishes to finish."

"I do this well enough, you won't have to wash this one."

"But you can't eat sin," I interrupted, "especially some-one else's."

Grandpa finished the crust. "No, I guess that's right. You can't eat someone else's sin. And Lord knows we all have enough of our own to worry about without trying to get at someone else's too."

"So whoever he was, he couldn't have been a real Sin Eater. He couldn't really eat sin."

"You remember that old story, Livia, come down from Erastus about the Sin Eater?"

"Sure."

"Come tell it."

"I can't tell it when I've got soap all over my arms."

"Well, towel it off and come tell Cole that story."

Now, Grandma wasn't much for telling stories. She knew that Grandpa dearly loved to tell them, and she loved to sit back and listen, watching him, loving his cantankerous self, not interrupting with what really happened. But now she came back to the table, her hands red from the hot water, and sat down next to Grandpa.

"It's a Christmas story really," she said, "about a time after the fire."

"After?" I asked.

"Don't interrupt, Cole. It's a story," said Grandpa.

"It's when the Sin Eater was living here, staying up in the hired man's room. He was helping out with chores to pay his keep, though it was winter and there wasn't much to do—milk, feed, muck out, mend some of the harnesses worn during the summer, fix up some of the stalls—the same as we do now. On Christmas Eve he'd been with the family, first to church, then calling, and it was just before midnight when they got back. Hieronymus sent Erastus out with the Sin Eater to check on the milkers one last time, to see if their water was frozen over.

"You know the kind of night when the air is so cold it feels like it's cracking, and the stars so keen they pierce? That's the kind of night it was. They didn't use the ell because they had to fetch one of the kerosene lanterns from the outside shed, and by the time they got to the barn to check on the milkers they were shivering. Even when he was an old man, Erastus remembered how cold that Christmas Eve was.

"Together they slid the door to. It didn't help much with the cold, but it did cut down some on the sound of the wind. The Sin Eater stamped the snow off his feet and slapped his sides. Erastus took off his cap and used it to brush the snow off his shoulders. By the yellow light of the lantern they looked like they were dancing, stepping to the hissing of the flame.

"'It'll be warmer down by the animals,' said Erastus.

"The Sin Eater nodded and motioned for Erastus to lead on. They climbed down the ladder to the milking stalls. When Erastus reached the bottom, the cows let him know that they weren't pleased with the light. It wasn't milking time yet, and they would rather be asleep. They set up such an annoyed mooing that you would have thought someone was being murdered.

"Erastus hung the lantern on the post. He ran his fingers in the water trough to make sure it wasn't iced over, and then slipped his hands under the twine of a bale, hefted it down, and slung it towards the stalls.

"And suddenly the cows were absolutely silent.

"He looked around. The Sin Eater had finally gotten to the bottom of the ladder and was just swinging off. And the cows were all staring at him, watching him as though they had never seen the like before. And then, well, Erastus knew that what happened next no one would ever believe if he told them. So he never did, outside the family.

"Slowly, one knee at a time, the three cows shrugged their great bodies to the ground and bowed before the Sin Eater."

Grandma finished and stood up to go back to the dishes.

"Grandma," I began, but she held up her hands.

"That's what Erastus said. I know that he was just a boy, and all excited about Christmas Eve, and probably pretty sleepy and all. But that's what he said. And he never changed his mind about it happening."

"Cows don't bow."

"Midnight of a Christmas Eve, who knows what can happen."

"But I thought that the Sin Eater died when his farm burned down."

"There's lots of stories about what happened up at the farm that night. None of them were true. His farm burned down, he needed a place to stay, and Hieronymus needed a hand. That's all there was."

"Not all," I answered. "Not if he could eat sin and was full of it."

"Oh, as for that," scoffed Grandpa, "who are we to judge?"

And that was the first time I knew who was buried beyond the two blank stones in the Emerson burial yard.

FIVE

Come September Grandpa drove me down to the John Greenleaf Whittier Middle School to register. It's probably true that every house has its own smell, but there's two places that smell the same no matter where they are or who uses them: a cow barn and a school. A cow barn has the smells of work: the warm breath of cows, the hay scent, the old hewn 8 × 8s, the neat's-foot oil softening the leather harnesses, the grainy smell of the feed. In a school the halls are filled with the scents of piney disinfectant, new paint on metal lockers, and polyurethane on sanded gym floors.

Mrs. Pluckett was one of those school principals who looked like she couldn't stand anyone wasting her time. She stood up smartly behind her desk when Grandpa and I came in, gave the kind of smile only a hassled administrator on the first day of school can give, thumped my hand up and down as if she had been waiting just for me to make her school complete, then sat down as quickly as she had stood.

"All your records were mailed in promptly." She smiled, and I took that as praise even though I had had nothing to do with it. "We just need your current address."

"He lives with us," supplied Grandpa.

"And your address?"

"Albion," said Grandpa, leaning back.

"Is there a street address?"

"No. Just Albion. That's how it's always been."

Mrs. Pluckett turned to me. I could tell that her tired enthusiasm was waning. It was going to be a long day and we were making it longer.

"Your parents are living with you as well?"

"His mother is deceased. His father was unable to come today."

Actually Dad hadn't been out of the hired man's room for three days, but I suppose Grandpa was technically correct.

"Your mother's name?" Mrs. Pluckett asked me.

"Hope Emerson Hallett," answered Grandpa.

Mrs. Pluckett looked startled for a moment, and stared hard at me. "Of course," she said, "I should have known." Then she shook her head as though to remind herself that time was a-wasting.

"You need to know anything else?" asked Grandpa.

"Thank you, Mr. Emerson. I think Cole and I can finish these forms up together, and then we'll get him a home-room and a schedule." She stood up and held out her hand. Grandpa wasn't used to being dismissed. If Mrs. Pluckett had been a deacon he would have been right after her. But I suppose he didn't want to start a fuss, this being my first day, so he stood up after just two or three seconds of hesitation, shook Mrs. Pluckett's hand, tousled my hair, and left, the glass door shutting silently behind him. The room was suddenly smaller.

"Now, Cole," said Mrs. Pluckett, "I think perhaps we'll put you in Mr. Shaw's homeroom. His is room 32 and he'll be your American history teacher as well." She wrote quickly on a form. "And the secretary just outside will have an envelope with your schedule in it." She finished writing, then looked at me as if trying to make up her mind. "I'm sorry about your mother."

I nodded.

"I knew her, you know. We grew up in John Whittier together, she and I, until I moved down to Boston."

"I didn't think this building was that old."

She sat back and started to laugh. "Well, Cole, I don't think I could make that into a compliment if I tried, so I won't. The old John Whittier burned down, and this was built the next year—the year I began as principal. You look like Hope. I suppose you have the Emerson face. I don't know if you'll be as quiet and gentle as she was, though. No one was as gentle as her. She wasn't the kind of person who liked field hockey at all."

"That's right," I said. "Gentle is a good word. Not always, but usually."

"Yes, not always," agreed Mrs. Pluckett. "There was one time in the eighth grade when Miss Cottrell had us memorize a John Greenleaf Whittier poem. We chose the titles from out of a hat. Your mother chose 'The Barefoot Boy' and was supposed to recite it in front of an auditorium full of parents. But she wouldn't do it. And day after day when time came to recite in front of the class, Miss Cottrell would insist that she recite and your mother would sit like a stone, not moving."

"How come?"

"Do you know how the poem reads? 'I was once a barefoot boy.' She knew she couldn't say that in front of us."

"So she never recited it."

"No, she did. On the night of the performance she walked to the front of the stage, curtsied, and announced that she would recite 'The Barefoot Girl.' She recited it perfectly, but ended with 'I was once a barefoot girl.' Your grandfather stood up and applauded, but when Miss Cottrell came onstage to lead her off, her face was red as a beet. For weeks afterwards, except when Miss Cottrell was around, we called her Barefoot Girl."

Mrs. Pluckett took off her glasses and laid them on her desk. She looked out the window. "It doesn't seem so very long ago," she said. "But you'd better go on to your homeroom."

The day went by in crowds and hollers and slamming lockers and armloads of books fresh from the printer, their pages still stuck together. Teachers called out lists of names in short staccatos, and I usually ended up somewhere in the middle. It seemed like I was playacting, as if I should be back in Philadelphia in a class that I knew, in a school that I knew. Except for Will in American history and gym, and Peter in algebra, I didn't know a single living soul in all that school.

Mrs. Pluckett had known my mother.

I was stunned by her story of "The Barefoot Girl." My mother had had a whole life I knew nothing about. There were people who could tell stories about her that I had never heard, and I didn't even know who they were. With each new class I looked at the teacher, wondering if this one, too, had known Hope Emerson and had been in the auditorium that night.

Everyone, that is, except Coach DuChenney. I knew

instinctively that he could never have known her. If every school smells the same, every school also has the same gym teacher. Coach DuChenney spent the period preaching the virtues of good eating and spurning "white death": salt, flour, and sugar, especially sugar. But the way his belt disappeared under his stomach suggested that the preaching was for our ears only. In the days that followed he made us sprint up and down the bleacher steps, though we doubted that he could even walk up without putting out a sweat. We did wind sprints, sit-ups fifty at a time, and track laps to make you weep. It was all conditioning with no game.

And he was mean. Will could have run seven laps to his one, but it made no difference. "You gonna play soccer for Whittier this year, Hurd, you better move your butt a lot faster than that!"

"Keep your knees down on the sit-ups! Down!"

"You call that flat-out running, Hallett? Flat-out? Do you know what that means?"

He must have wanted to be hated. It was the only explanation for why he drove us to it with such glee. He could make us hate him while we practiced corner kicks, while we ran cross-country, while we played lacrosse, while we lined up, for heaven's sake.

But, most especially, he could make us hate him while we climbed the Rope.

It was on a Monday that we came into the gym to find the Rope dangling from the ceiling, circling just a bit over a single thin mat. Its end was frayed and unraveling; generations of duct tape held it together. It smelled like old lawn clippings.

The Rope hung down a hundred feet or so from the steel girders above the gym floor. Standing at the bottom and looking up, I thought that it may as well have disappeared into the clouds for all the likelihood I had of climbing to the top. In the few minutes of free time we had before Coach DuChenney drilled us into squads, we all tried our hands at the slick hemp, hefting ourselves up. Will, though, shot baskets.

Coach DuChenney lined up the squads so that the Rope hung between us, swaying just a bit with the world's spin. "No exercises today," he said slowly, staring down at his clipboard. "You'll need your energy for the Rope," and when the words finished echoing in the gym he looked up the length, shook his head, turned to us, and shook his head again as if he felt sorry for what he was about to make us do. Of course, he didn't.

He called the first name on his clipboard. "Bowditch."

Nate Bowditch could run like a deer, swim like a fish, and jump like a gazelle. He could stretch his thin self so tall he only had to give a little hop to reach a basketball net with his thin, bony fingers. But looking up at the Rope, he knew there was no way in creation he could climb it.

"A running leap, Bowditch. Hell, you can do that. Catch it high, wrap those long legs around, and scoot on up."

He tried. He ran up over the mat, leapt up, grabbed the Rope, slid down six or seven inches, then desperately wrapped his legs around the twitching rope so that he wouldn't slide farther and burn his hands.

"Hurd," called Coach DuChenney, "hold the bottom." Will did. "Climb on up, Bowditch," Coach ordered. "You're halfway there already."

77

Nate knew that he was nowhere near halfway. He also knew his hands were raw and getting rawer all the time. And he also knew that his arms weren't going to pull him any higher. "Watch out, Will," he called, and Will rolled away as he let go and fell like a scarecrow to the floor.

For a moment Coach DuChenney said nothing; he looked down at his clipboard and we could all see him drawing a large *X* through Nate's name. Then "Carpenter," he announced. "Hurd, you stay at the bottom."

He went through all sixteen of us, one by one, his directions always the same. And we ran up, stretched out our arms as high as we could, caught the Rope, and hung there. The thing coiled like a snake around our legs. I made it as high as the basketball hoops before my arms gave out and the Rope started to open up my hands.

"Waleski," bellowed Coach DuChenney. Ian Waleski walked up to the Rope, a silver crucifix showing through his shirt. Ian was the only kid in John Greenleaf Whittier Middle School who reminded us that not everyone came from old New England stock. The Waleskis had been around Albion for less than a generation, a family with a Polish father and a French-Quebec mother, so Ian grew up with stretched accents and exaggerated vowels— sounds none of us could make, even when he tried to teach us. He ate exotic lunches: spicy meats with thick layers of rough bread, sliced vegetables whose names none of us knew, yogurt, pastries filled with raspberry jellies. He was as thin as Nate Bowditch but short, so he didn't look all spindly. And he was Catholic.

Albion, founded by second-generation Puritans, had never had a Catholic church. The closest one was in

Andover. When the Waleskis came to town, everyone wondered how to welcome them. Miss Cottrell suggested that it was none of the business of the Ladies Welcome Society of Albion Grace Church of the Holy Open Bible, which was, after all, Protestant. So no arrangements were made for the usual welcoming call. In the end, Grandma and Mrs. Dowdle and Mrs. Hurd went calling by themselves, never figuring that most of the hour would be spent in long silences, since Mrs. Waleski could speak no English. "I'm not sure we did much good," Grandma later told Grandpa, "but those pastries she served us!"

In school, we never talked about God and such, that being the stuff of Sunday. And besides, we pretty much all went to the same church and pretty much believed in the same things. There wasn't much to say. But Ian, being Catholic, seemed to have a whole mysterious other life completely apart from us, a life filled with incense, statues, rosaries, dark-pillared churches, incantations, confessional booths, and long-robed priests. But aside from Wednesday, when he left school early for catechism, and Sunday morning, when he and his family drove down to Andover for early mass, it was a life he never let show.

He stood at the bottom of the Rope, feeling it with his hands, looking up to the ceiling. "Go ahead, Ian," whispered Will.

"You waiting for the pope to invite you up the Rope?" hollered Coach DuChenney.

Silence in the gym. Absolute silence.

Ian's face set. He jumped high, caught the Rope, and with six long pulls was higher than anyone had made it so far.

"Keep going, Waleski. A Hail Mary or two will get you up."

Ian stopped dead. I don't know if he would have made it any higher; none of us knew. He loosed his legs and very slowly came down, hand over hand, smooth and determined. He lowered himself to the bottom and turned to face Coach DuChenney, who put down his clipboard and folded his arms across his chest.

"Ian," warned Will.

Ian stepped towards the coach.

"Ian," said Will again, "hold the Rope for me."

Ian's arms were still at his sides, his hands clenched. He walked slowly until he stood directly in front of Coach DuChenney, so close they could breathe on each other.

"You have something to say to me, Waleski?"

Ian's knee came up hard against him. We had all been watching his hands, but they didn't move. Just his knee. DuChenney's face opened and he went white. He thrust his hands to his middle, doubled at the waist, and lost his breakfast all over the gym floor. Ian ran into the locker room, his face smeared with sudden tears.

No one knew what to do—go after Ian or help the gagging gym teacher. So we stood, transfixed, watching in fascination, the Rope swinging back and forth between us all.

When Will and I came out of the locker room later, Coach DuChenney was closed in his office and the mess was cleaned up. "Will," I pointed out, "you never had a chance to climb the Rope."

He smiled like he had just landed the biggest trout in the Great Hosmer, handed me his books, and sat down on the gym floor, directly beneath the Rope, his legs straight.

And then, using just his arms and keeping his legs jutting out at a perfect angle from the Rope, he climbed, his arms like cables doing easily what they were supposed to do, until he reached the ceiling and slapped the girder. Then he slid down like he was oiled, his legs still out, until he sat on the gym floor again. He held back the laugh breaking from inside him, took his books, and pranced snootily toward the gym door—until I tackled him from behind.

We left the gym as the loudspeaker crackled and an electric voice summoned Ian Waleski to the Middle School office immediately.

No one saw Ian again for the rest of that day. We never heard what went on between Ian and Mrs. Pluckett, but there was no end of ideas. "Arrested," said Alice Fiske. "Definitely arrested. You can't hit a teacher without being arrested. You watch. Anytime now, Mr. Fordham will come around with some sort of warrant." None of us ever told her where Ian hit DuChenney; it hurt too much to say.

Will figured that Ian would have detention for the rest of his life. We all thought that Ian would be suspended at least through Christmas, and Peter said it would be for the year.

So we were all shocked when he walked into school the next day.

He was like someone set apart: He had hit a teacher. He walked like a condemned man who knew he would be executed in a week, never meeting anyone's eyes, only half answering a nervous "hello." He moved alone like the air was charged around him with terrible guilt.

Until noon.

While Mrs. Duffin worked through one of those algebra problems where two people take it into their heads to drive off in different directions at different speeds, I looked out the window and saw Will and Ian sitting in the playground, eating lunch, Will pointing all around the yard as though planning an attack. Which he was, I found out after school.

"Cole," he said, "do you know what Pluckett is making Ian do?"

"I wonder what she's making DuChenney do."

Will ignored that. "She's making Ian spend every Friday afternoon raking leaves around the school. Every single Friday until all the leaves are gone."

I looked around. In the schoolyard, the maples were shaking off their leaves like dogs shaking off water. They fell in heaps, yellow hills giving the yard a whole new geography, so thick I could have walked in them up to my knees. I groaned. "He must have told her what DuChenney said."

"I don't think he did. So now he's got all this raking."

I unchained my bicycle and looked at the leaves coming down as fast as the wind could cart them off the branches. "That will take forever."

"Well." Will smiled. "Maybe not."

That Friday afternoon, Coach DuChenney's second-period gym class formed up after school in the playground, rakes in hand, and listened to Will assign each squad a sector. It took a little over an hour for four squads to rake up the maple leaves into a pile higher than any two of us. And just as we finished we heard the smooth chugging of Grandpa on the McCormick, driving into the schoolyard pulling the trailer, sided with long boards, behind. He pulled up to the pile.

"Let's get 'em in," he called over the engine, and with shouts we scooped the leaves up in rakes and piled them into the trailer, filling it to the top. Then we all jumped in, falling softly to the bottom, covering one another with leaves until they were in our eyes and mouths. Swaying with the motion of the trailer as the McCormick pulled out to River Road towards the farm—"Git up!"—and to the fire pit, we drove to where Grandma stood with the stock of sharpened sticks, two bags of marshmallows, and a tall pot filled with cider, a screen over the top.

"You boys best get those leaves burning," Grandma said.

Of course you weren't allowed to burn leaves anymore in Albion proper, but Grandpa figured that the law didn't apply to him, living outside of town. He didn't stop even when Mr. Fordham drove out in his black-and-white to remind us that the law was countywide.

"Frank," Grandpa said, "how long you been upholding the law in this county fair?"

"Three years now, going on four."

"And how long do you figure I've been abiding by the law in this county, more or less?"

"I suppose a long time."

"You suppose right. So when your upholding catches up to my abiding, I'll worry about burning leaves." Mr. Fordham shook his head at this, not quite following. He thought on it for a while until Grandma handed him a browned marshmallow. Then he helped the rest of us cart leaves from the trailer to the fire; he had to shake them off his sticky fingers.

We looked forward to Friday afternoons from that time on. It got to be that we had to tell other kids that they couldn't help, not even if they brought their own rakes—not even if they brought their own marshmallows.

By late September all of the leaves of Albion had started their turning, blushing and gushing into reds and golds and yellows. Grandma said they were putting on airs; Grandpa watched the fields and whistled softly. You can't tell someone what fall leaves look like in New Hampshire. In fact, you can't even really remember what they look like from one year to the next. Every fall they throw a surprise party, and suddenly you remember what you've forgotten. And it's not just the colors. It's the cooler breezes that draw across the leaves, making them shiver. It's the cold dew that beads on them and wets the arm of your jacket. It's the dusty smell when they're dry in the afternoon. And it's the thick smoke that coils up from them when they burn just before suppertime.

After the first hard frost shriveled up the tomato vines, beheaded most of the flowers, and killed everything in the garden except the brussels sprouts (which deserved to get killed), the leaves began to fall like paratroopers, cutting down through the air in swathes, settling without noise onto the grass. They fell in the town Commons, circling the feet of the Civil War memorial like a wreath. They fell by the ledges, where the water was now too cold to swim in, and they circled round and round in the pools until finally washed downstream. They fell across the front yard of Grandpa's house, where we all three raked them up, threw them at one another, raked them up again, and finally burned them, usually on Sunday afternoons so people from town could drive out and smell the smoke-filled air that reminded them of what they were missing.

All of the houses around the Commons were fronted by oaks and maples that had been there since before the town was founded, and they threw down their leaves every day for about six weeks. They were, Will said, a business opportunity, and he and Peter and I founded Lawn Constructors, Inc. Will and Peter had to put in extra hours at Kaye's on Mondays and Tuesdays to make up for being away on Fridays, so we started slowly, with only a few yards. But once hard frosts were coming most every day, Kaye closed down after lunch, and we could expand.

By the first week of October we had three regular customers for every day after school—except on Fridays, which we spent at the schoolyard, and Wednesdays, which we spent at Miss Cottrell's. Hers wasn't the biggest yard on the Commons, but it had the most front bushes to trap leaves, and the most flowerbeds where leaves had to be pulled out by hand, and the most intricate wrought-iron fence that took something like forever to rake around.

And it had Miss Cottrell. She figured that Lawn Constructors, Inc., needed as much supervision as she could stand to give, and she could stand plenty. "Don't leave those oak leaves there, they'll yellow up the grass just as quick as can be and the lawn will look like Mrs. Dowdle's, which has never been the same since she left that pile of dead leaves right in the middle of her lawn all the winter long"—a breath—"and when the snow melted there was a yellow spot just like a stain and nothing she could do about it except sod it over and you know how much that costs."

On Saturdays when we weren't raking, I had to help get the farm ready for winter. In the morning we'd drive into the Feed and Grain to stockpile up, loading the forty-pound sacks into the pickup and later lugging them up to the barn loft. Anne, Emily, and Charlotte watched with big chocolate eyes, sometimes shaking their heads. The Frisian pawed at the straw, sending out a flubbery neigh and poking his big muzzle at the sacks as we carried them up, and stamping at the sound of our steps overhead.

Outside we dug in the garden for the last time, finally picking all the brussels sprouts and harvesting the turnips. We layered the rows thick with manure and plowed it under, along with a dusting of snow from the night before. Grandpa liked to look at his garden when it was growing and green, but there was a pleasure too in seeing it bedded down and ready for next year. Grandma felt the same about the cemetery, where she'd pruned the dead flowers, clipped any stray patches, and tucked the moss right up to the chins of the stones, ready for a winter's sleep.

By the time the oaks were starting to fling their leaves down, it was so cold that Miss Cottrell had to put on two thick sweaters to supervise—but she didn't seem to mind. The last time we were to be there she kept us till about dark, when we could no longer see the leaves blowing over from Mrs. Dowdle's lawn. Snow was in the air, and the wind chilled the sweat on the back of our necks and numbed the ends of our fingers. It was good to see Peter's father park across the street in their pickup. "Miss Cottrell," he greeted, giving a slight nod.

"Walford. Isn't it a shame that some people don't rake their leaves?" she said, pointing with her cane. "As if it isn't awful enough to let your own lawn go to ruin without taking a neighbor's with it; I tell you, Walford, that if some people kept track of their own yard, these boys would have been done an hour ago or maybe more."

"I suppose that's true," Mr. Gealy said, "and I expect if there was light enough I'd be able to see what a fine job they've done on your lawn. But it's time I got these boys home to supper. It's a school night, and you know how that is."

Miss Cottrell looked up into the sky, dark except for the flakes hovering in the air until they caught the wind and spurted away. "I suppose it is too dark to do any more raking now," she admitted, "and it is a school night." With a wave of her cane she dismissed us all like a queen her courtiers.

We loaded the bikes into the pickup and jostled into the cab. Peter's dad leaned down and kissed him on the top of his head, and suddenly my stomach gripped.

"Cole," Mr. Gealy said, "I called your folks. You'd be welcome to supper with us tonight."

"You talked to Dad?"

"Your grandmother."

"Okay. I'd like to come."

"Good. I'd ask you too, Will, but your mom said you had company tonight."

"Did she say who?"

"Nope."

"That's bad," said Will, sitting back. "It means she didn't want me to know and I'll have to get dressed up and dinner will last forever."

"Sorry, Will," laughed Mr. Gealy. "I really am."

We dropped Will off and watched him shuffle towards his house, then headed back through town. Peter's family lived on the far side of Albion, close to the Chickwolnepy River, so when we got out of the pickup we could hear the water over the rocks singing its forever song. At the sound of the truck the door opened and yellow light poured out across the yard. Mrs. Gealy stood by the door, and behind her Peter's baby sisters. They squealed when he came in and each took him by a knee. He walked with them hugging his legs, thumping like a giant around the warm kitchen. "Fee, fie, foe, fum."

"Enough, girls." Mrs. Gealy smiled, peeling them off. Then she placed a hand by Peter's cheek and patted him once. "And you, Cole," she said, turning to me, "you're welcome here." And she bent down and kissed me lightly on the forehead. The kiss hung there, burning, for a long time.

I wasn't sure what to expect at supper. Mr. Gealy's prayer was short, one you could tell he'd said many times. He looked around, held his hands out wide, and then closed his eyes: "Bless us Father, and these Thy many good gifts." He wasn't talking about just the food.

And then, such a chattering. Gravied beef and garden beans with almonds and spiced tomatoes and parslied red potatoes being passed back and forth, the giggles of the twins and the deep laughter of Mr. Gealy; Peter's imitation

88

of Miss Cottrell with her cane and the stifled laughter of his mother—"Peter, you shouldn't imitate people"; and the cries that greeted the apple tart and its flaky cinnamon shell. Lord. And then, when the girls ran off, the steam of coffee twining up into the air (my first cup), and finally Peter nodding to me to help check on the woodstove, and his parents reaching out to hold each other's hands as we left.

The Glenwood stove squatted amiably in the old parlor of the farmhouse, the room where the minister sat when he called. Now the room was filled with the stuff of everyday life. One corner propped up a stack of the twins' games, and I wondered how they could ever get one off the bottom without scattering the tower. The table in the middle of the room held a jigsaw, the frame and most of the city scene at the bottom all done, the sky pieces all in a pile. Shelves of books spread across the walls, stopping short of the woodstove, bulging down the centers with sets of Dickens, Twain, Scott, and Jules Verne. Pillows had shuffled themselves all across the floor, open books beside them, some marked, most of them turned facedown to keep the page.

While Peter tended to the Glenwood, I followed the line of photographs set just inside the parlor door. They were the old sepia ones of serious-faced families, just like Mrs. Dowdle's. Most were wedding pictures, some of family reunions with everyone gathered on the porch of a clapboard house.

And one of the Sin Eater.

I knew him right away, though there was no beard this time. He stood holding a baby in each arm, an older son by his knee gripping his mother's hand. They stood in front of a whitewashed cottage, and beyond that the sea rounded off the horizon. No one looked at the camera; they stared beyond it, looking towards something that was coming, or maybe going.

"That's Thomas Gealy and his family," said Peter, popping stove-length logs into the Glenwood. Some smoke escaped from the open door and drifted up to the ceiling. "He was the first Gealy over here, from Wales. That's their leave-taking picture."

"Leave-taking?"

"He left his wife and kids in Wales to come set up a life here, in Albion. He bought the farm and everything. But by the time they got over, he had died. Some fever that no one knew how to break."

"But his family stayed, even though he was dead."

"Obviously, since I'm here."

"I guess. Will and I went up to his farm the night we camped out."

"I go up there sometimes. I wish the house was still there, and everything in it. It could tell a lot about him."

"And how he was a Sin Eater."

Mr. Gealy came into the room and chafed his hands in the heat of the Glenwood as Peter closed its door. "It's funny how things keep on," he said. "Thomas Gealy left Wales to escape that life. He was the first Sin Eater in his village to ever marry and have children, and he didn't want them to live there, with their father a Sin Eater. And maybe becoming Sin Eaters themselves. So he left. But he couldn't leave it behind. Even here, that's how he's still remembered."

90

"But, Mr. Gealy, I don't think anyone can eat sin. Not really eat it."

"I'm not sure how he did it. It's a gift, you know, what he did." He held his hands out, as if he wanted to show Peter and me something. "He healed. Sometimes people would bake bread and say their sin was in it, and they'd leave it on the windowsill or the doorstep and he would come by and take it and people would feel healed, like they'd rid themselves of something. Sometimes they would come out to talk, just talk. And they would leave whatever they needed to leave and not have to carry it anymore. He gave them the chance to let go of their hurt. And for that he lived alone on the edge of a Welsh marsh most of his life."

"Until he came here," Peter said.

"Until he came here. But even here, once people found out he'd been a Sin Eater, he had to live out on the edge of town. And the stories that got around! Meeting the devil out in a storm."

"How did word get around here?" I asked.

Mr. Gealy shrugged. "I suppose he ate sin once and that was enough for word to get around. Why don't you show Cole that letter?" Peter crossed the room and pulled out an old beaten black album. He spread it across the jigsaw puzzle and flipped through a few pages—more sepia photographs—until he came to a letter pasted in. He let his finger slide down the slant of the letters until he reached the last paragraph "Read this," he said. So I did.

The house is gone, and the barn. God knows if I should return to you or you come to me. Sometimes I

wonder why God has brought me to this place, and
yet when I look at the dawn on the mountains and see
how beautiful it is, I cannot but think that this is the
place God has intended for us all along. And in any
case, there is the Task to do here one more time. One
more time before it is done forever. I know you will
object, dearheart, and say that the Task is part of the
old ways and not the new. But it needs doing here—
one last time—for two who would love each other if
they could. And after that, it is done for all time, and
all that will be left to do is to love you.

I finished the letter and shivered despite the heat coming from the Glenwood. "Whose sin did he eat?" I asked.

"I don't know. No one knows."

"Peter, you remember how in the church Will said no
one knows where he's buried?"

"Yeah."

"I think I know."

Mr. Gealy drove us up River Road that night in frosted
air, the stars perfect pinpricks above us, the last of the
leaves brushed across the road by the rush of air as we
drove by. When we reached home, I went with Peter and
Mr. Gealy to the Emerson Burial Yard and stood in back
of the single stone: WHO ARE WE TO JUDGE? Mr. Gealy
took off his glove and rubbed his finger against the worn
stone, back and forth, trying to feel the letters since he
could not see them. Then he stood up, nodded, and
turned to me, his eyes dark. "Thank you, Cole," he said.
"Thank you for tending to him. And for finding him."

"It's hard to imagine why anyone would want to be a Sin Eater," I said, looking at the cold, lonely stone.

"No reason but grace," said Mr. Gealy. "That's the way it always is." He reached out and shook my hand, hard, one man to another. Peter waved, then followed his father back to the pickup. I watched them drive off.

No light showed up in the hired man's room when I went in. I sat in the best room with Grandma and Grandpa while they read old *Reader's Digest*s and the phonograph played hymns, Grandma rocking to their measures, pausing only when the scratches went against the rhythm. I studied Andrew Jackson's presidency for Mr. Shaw's test tomorrow until Grandma sent me to bed. "A clear mind's the best preparation, and the only way to get that is a good night's rest."

Scrunched up against the cold sheets, the soft weight of the down comforter over me, I looked up into the blackness and put my hand to my forehead. Mrs. Gealy's kiss was still there, still warm.

SIX

THE PORTSMOUTH COUNTY FAIR fixed the calendar to the year like a pin through a wheel, spinning the seasons around itself. Come spring, gardeners planted with the fair in mind, manuring and choosing the sunniest patch for competition vegetables. In the summer, they chose what looked to be their finest, propping up spindly green tomato branches or nursing a pumpkin tendril into a bowl of milk. In fall, the harvest. And come winter, winners opened the kitchen cupboards to look at the blue ribbons tacked inside; those who didn't win this year looked at fading ribbons from years past and made resolutions about the next harvest.

Towards the end of October I began biking down to Albion and picking up Will and Peter early in the morning; together we'd head out to the fairgrounds, where tents rose like mountains out of the plains, and the long exhibition halls filled up with stock. Fresh sawdust, dark red with the dew, covered the horse corral, and new white paint announced that the popcorn and hot dog stands were just about ready. Hawkers tested their wheels and rides, harassed carpenters ran to shore up stalls that hadn't wintered well, and sound systems squeaked out "one-two-three, one-two-three, testing."

Just the smell of canvas and sawdust and horses and cows in the early morning frost was almost enough to keep us away from school. DuChenney was another reason. He was cause enough.

He never spoke to Ian Waleski anymore; in fact, he hardly spoke to any of us, hollering out directions like a dog barking at nothing. He knew about the Friday afternoons, though he never would have said anything to us about them. He decided instead that he would hunker down into himself and act as if we were hardly there. So no more touch football, no more basketball. No equipment ever left the locker room. Instead, we ran laps. Again and again around the quarter-mile track, we ran laps.

No one ever complained. We let Ian pace us around the track, following him through the morning cold for two or three miles at a clip, not looking at DuChenney, who was not looking at us. That fall, we all improved our wind.

When winter started to hint that it was coming, DuChenney never let up. Every day we ran laps, even when the track was slick from a freezing rain, even when snowflakes blew thinly through the air. DuChenney stood outside, wearing an air force coat, fur around his face, a Styrofoam cup of coffee steaming in his hands, not watching us.

It was good to have the fair to think about while we ran around the track, the sound of gravel in our ears, the chill of the air on our cheeks. Grandma had been baking apple pies for it, experimenting with new recipes so Grandpa and I had a new apple pie every night, each with a new set of spices.

"What do you think?" Grandma would ask.

"Perfect," said Grandpa.

"Nothing better," I agreed.

"I wonder if the nutmeg goes with the cinnamon quite so well as it should," said Grandma.

Opening day of the fair, Grandma was as nervous as I'd ever seen her. At breakfast, Grandpa talked about leaving early so we could get a parking space close to the entrance.

"No," said Grandma firmly. We both looked at her, surprised. "We can't go until that Edith Cottrell has brought her pie."

Grandpa put his coffee on the table and sat back in his chair. "Olivia Emerson, what on earth are you talking about?"

"We're not going until Edith Cottrell has put her pie on display and written down the recipe in front of the judges."

"And when is that going to be?"

"Sometime before noon. If we get there just about quarter of, that should work out fine."

We arrived at the Big Top at ten of, Grandma holding her apple pie underneath a checkered red cloth. Miss Cottrell was nowhere to be seen; her pie was not on the table.

"I guess we waited for nothing," said Grandpa. "Edith Cottrell isn't going to bring a pie."

Grandma looked around, worried. She waited five more minutes, then brought her pie to the judges' table and entered it. She wrote the recipe out on an index card and set it in front of the pie pan, turning the pie until it looked just so.

"You always did make the best apple pies, Olivia." This from Miss Cottrell, carrying in her entry at the very stroke of noon. "Such a perfectly brown crust. And you used nutmeg! I wonder if it will clash too much with the cinnamon."

Grandma smiling tightly. Grandpa wiping his hand across his mouth.

"Results at four o'clock," hollered the judge.

I met Will and Peter at the exhibition halls.

The sawdust in the halls was ankle deep, so we felt like we were walking through a marsh. It absorbed the sound;

even a curly-haired hoof striking against the ground was muted. In most of the stalls—some decorated with the ribbons of past fairs—brushes were stroking across broad backs, grooming away any bit of mud, any hint of sweat.

Horses liked Will. He could touch them once and they would recognize a kindred spirit, shoving warm, soft muzzles into his cupped hands. With me, they didn't react much. They just snorted, stamped a front hoof, and turned back to their feed. It was like that with The Frisian too. Will could walk into the barn and the horse would turn frisky, trotting up and leaning down to be scratched behind the ears like a dog. But for me, just snorts—never mind that I had been the one to feed him since the beginning of summer.

Eating popcorn, then cotton candy, then more popcorn, then chili dogs, then fried dough sprinkled with sugar and cinnamon, we walked through halls of long-eared rabbits, bleating goats with budded horns, drowsy sheep, and warm cows chewing, chewing, chewing the hay they'd ripped from bales. We hurried past the pig pens. We tried one roller coaster, ignoring the warning sign: "Some people may feel discomfort if they have recently eaten before taking this ride." We shouldn't have ignored the sign. It was more than discomfort.

Everywhere, the air was filled with flashing lights, piping calliope music, the smell of cotton candy and frying fat, and the cries of the hawkers.

"Get your red hots here. Red hots. Get your red hots."

"Doggie! Doggie! Doggie! Doggie!"

"Three tries for a quarter. Three for two bits. Just two bits. Three tries for a quarter."

97

And then we came to the slammer hammer and Coach DuChenney.

There's something about a teacher outside of school that seems wrong; he didn't belong there, not at the Portsmouth County Fair. Smoking a cigarette and clutching a beer, he watched each contestant heft the mallet into the air and bring it down with all the force he could muster. But the weight never made it even halfway up the pole, never close to the silent bell on top. And with every failure, DuChenney smirked.

Before we knew enough to look away, our eyes met and burned. Then he turned and got in line. We could not leave; we stood in the middle of the path, the crowd parting around us, and waited for Coach DuChenney to make his bid.

He tossed his cigarette to the ground and stamped it out with his heel. Finishing the beer in one gulp, he crumpled the cup into a ball and threw it deftly into a trash can fifteen feet away, a perfect swish. He took off his jacket and tied the sleeves—barely—just below his waist. Then he rolled up his shirtsleeves and began flexing his arms, warming up.

It was his turn.

He took the mallet and held it straight out, like a baseball bat, like he was judging its weight. Five, ten seconds he held it straight out, and it never trembled. Then, slowly, he put the head to the ground and cupped his hands around his mouth to spit in them. Slowly he picked up the mallet again, looking over his shoulder to see if we were still watching. He heaved it up, high over his back, angled straight out from the front leg he'd planted in the worn earth. Then it came down, crashing through the air like a locomotive, hurtling like a bull towards the slammer.

It missed by a good six inches and buried itself in the ground.

Stunned silence. It was as if the whole fair had suddenly come to a halt.

"Damn," said Will under his breath.

The hawker took the mallet from DuChenney's hands, but he didn't move. He just slumped there, all bent over, like an actor playing out a death scene. The hawker touched his shoulder and whispered to him to move away, let the next guy try. But DuChenney did not move.

"Give him another try," Will suddenly yelled. "Let him try again. C'mon Coach, you can do this."

The hawker raised his eyebrows at us, shrugged his shoulders, and handed the mallet back to DuChenney. He reached out, looked back at us for a moment, then took it and squared his shoulders. He heaved the mallet up again, paused at the upswing, and came thudding down on the slammer.

There was no doubt from the moment he hit it that the bell would ring. The weight skidded up the pole like it was on butter, racing hot into the sky. Before DuChenney straightened, the bell sounded clear and loud, announcing a glorious deed. The rest of the contestants waiting in line clapped and cheered. But DuChenney said nothing to them. He stepped aside, unrolled his sleeves, and walked over to us, putting his jacket on.

"Basketball practice starts Monday, boys," he said, and then walked on down the midway.

Peter punched me on the shoulder, laughing.

"What are you grinning at?" I swung at him but he danced away, running backwards through the crowd.

"Our laps are over," he crowed, arms up in the air. And I knew he was right.

Out along the midway, on the other side of the fair and past the exhibition halls, the arena for the tractor pull sprawled its muddy self. Grandpa thought tractor pulls were barbaric: "Tearing apart tractors, trying to make them do what they were never intended to do." When Grandma asked him why he went to the pull at every fair, he mumbled something about how important it was for the righteous to keep an eye on the sinners. Then he'd head out to the barn to lube something or other.

"Cantankerous old man," she'd mutter, smiling as she watched him go.

When Peter, Will, and I got to the arena, Grandpa was standing by the fence, one foot pushing down the first crossbeam, his arms elbowed up on the top. Grandma fidgeted behind him. For all she knew, at that very moment the judges were cutting into her pie and smelling the nutmeg and cinnamon coming up through the crust. She hoped that Miss Cottrell wasn't there to wrinkle her nose at the clashing spices.

I had to touch Grandpa on the shoulder to let him know we were there, what with the tractors roaring out their combustions, ripping up the ground with grooved wheels, and sending mud spattering clear across the field. Slowly they lugged long sledges, dragging a load of cement blocks towards a finish line marked by bright ribbons. Supporters in the stands were calling out and screaming, but you couldn't hear anything above the tractors, not until they both got fully across the line and shut down.

Clowns rushed out to pull the linchpins and free the tractors from their loads. Two new tractors appeared at the entrance to the arena and chugged across, wheeling around and backing towards the sledges. "Wheel around a couple of more times like that and they'll start to bow their axles," Grandpa said out loud. "Fool business."

Grandma was still fidgeting.

"Olivia, there's nothing that can be done about it now. It doesn't matter if you put in one pinch of nutmeg or fifty. That pie is sitting there and the judges are eating it."

"I just bet that Edith Cottrell has entered an apple pie again."

"You know you make the best pies in all of Albion. Lord, in all the state."

"You just have to say that."

"I don't have to say anything! You ask Pastor Hurd if I say things just because I have to. You ask anyone."

Grandma's face softened into a smile, and she laid her hand on his arm.

We watched six more tractor pulls, the sledges dragged back and forth across the arena, the tractors digging ruts into the deepening mud, the times posted, the smell of diesel over everything.

Then Henry Cooper drove into the arena with his new John Deere.

With all the ripping and roaring that had been going on, Mr. Cooper's tractor stood out there like it didn't belong. The suspension on those wheels took the ruts as if they were smooth grass. The engine hummed along like a choir singing a prelude, easy and slow, knowing there was some work ahead but not worried about it. Mr. Cooper drove close to the fence, and the sun glinted off the green and yellow metal, and the crowd grew quiet to see. This beautiful tractor sang soft, moved easy, and looked strong enough to pull the state of New Hampshire right off the map.

Mr. Cooper backed the tractor towards the sledge.

"Henry, what damn fool thing are you doing?" Grandpa clambered over the fence and landed deep in the mud. "Henry," he hollered, pulling his feet through the mud.

By now the tractors had started to roar like warriors pounding their chests, so we couldn't hear Grandpa anymore. But you could pretty well tell what he was hollering about. He jabbed his finger back and forth along Mr. Cooper's machine, kicked at its tires, held his hands over the engine, and pointed to the sledge. Then he stood with his hands on his hips, glaring at Mr. Cooper, who had pushed his hat back and was looking sort of helpless. He spread his arms wide and shrugged his shoulders. Grandpa turned, shaking his head.

But as Mr. Cooper settled into his seat, watching for the flag from the judge's platform, Grandpa didn't come back to the fence. He went behind the tractor and pulled the linchpin from the sledge.

It's hard to say exactly what happened next. Folks told it different ways afterwards. And Mr. Cooper kept claiming he didn't know that Grandpa was back there. But as soon as the judge dropped his flag, Mr. Cooper thrust his machine forward with the throttle wide open. That tractor leaped full in the air like a pheasant flushed out by a dog, Mr. Cooper clutching the wheel kind of desperately. It came down fifteen yards away, its wheels spinning like comets, and when they hit the ground they sent a blizzard of thick, black mud straight back on Grandpa so that there was not a spot on him that was not completely covered. You could hear his holler even over the tractors.

By the time Mr. Cooper could reach past the centrifugal force and get his hand to the gearshift, his tractor had covered the arena, taken out three sections of fencing, and knocked down one pole on the judge's stand, leaving it sloping down crazily. With one hand the judge was holding on to the handrail around the stand; with the other he held up a black flag: Contestant Disqualified.

We weren't quite sure what to do with Grandpa. Grandma said he should go on home and get cleaned up but Grandpa wasn't about to climb into his pickup with all that mud on him.

"Then, Hiram, you'll just have to hose yourself down over by the exhibition halls." And that's what we did. Grandpa walked along the midway, his back straight and head held high, daring anyone to say a thing to him. The mud was starting to dry a bit and flake off, so you could see patches of him, but mostly he was covered. He walked with his arms held away from his body and his legs wide.

We found a hose behind the goat hall and Grandpa tested it on his hand.

"This is cold," he complained.

Grandma showed no sympathy. "If you hadn't tried to interfere, you wouldn't be in this mess now."

"That fool Henry Cooper."

"It's not his fault you pulled that pin."

"It's his fault I was in there at all."

"Cantankerous old coot!"

"You take these boys and go see to your pie," Grandpa said.

"I'll meet you there then," and she turned towards the Big Top, dragging us with her. We made it past the exhibition halls, out of sight of Grandpa, before the laughter that we'd been holding back burst out of our guts. We leaned against one another, Grandma squealing high and tears running out of her eyes. If we hadn't heard the P.A. system, we might have missed getting back for the pie judging.

Perfect quiet when we got to the Big Top. The smell of sawdust and sweat. Three judges going over the list one more time. Tables with rows of pies, all sorted by fruit: apple, strawberry and strawberry-rhubarb, blueberry, preserved peach, huckleberry. A chocolate pie on one table, all alone—Mrs. Hurd's. She never came to the fair, partly because she wasn't sure it was proper for a reverend's wife, and partly because she couldn't stand the suspense of the competition. Will picked up the chocolate pie ribbon for her every year.

We stood just on the edge of the crowd. "I don't suppose it matters if I win or lose," Grandma said, "but if Edith Cottrell takes first place with an apple pie, I don't want to be trapped up front with her."

The head judge stood up, his black suit starting to show the heat. He cleared his throat, then called over the heads of the crowd. "We'll begin with the strawberry and strawberry-rhubarb category. Third place and the green ribbon goes to Mrs. Joanna Wight."

Polite applause scattered around the crowd.

"Second place and the red ribbon to Mrs. Bea Cooper."

Louder applause this time.

"And first place and the blue ribbon of the Portsmouth County Fair to Coach Louis DuChenney."

Dead silence.

Coach DuChenney walked through the crowd with a beaming smile. In fact, looking at him, I wondered if I had ever seen him smile before. He came up on stage, and the judge handed him the blue ribbon and then held Coach's pie up into the air.

"I never would have thought it," said Grandma. Will, Peter, and I looked at one another. We never would have thought it either.

The judges announced the preserved peach category next, and Mrs. Gealy took second place. Grandma was just about hopping back and forth by this time, her hands folding over each other like they weren't even a part of her. But once they announced the apple pie category, she stood absolutely still and set her face.

Up to now, people had been polite, but this was the major contest. These were apple pies, not some sweet dandy fruit. These were the recipes handed down since before the state was settled, and no one joked or laughed. Even the sawdust seemed to settle down as the judge straightened his tie and vest.

"Third place and the green ribbon to Mrs. Alice Duffin." A sudden squeal of delight pierced the quiet, and the crowd let Mrs. Duffin through. For apple pies, all three winners went up on stage.

"Second place to Kaye Cottrell." The regulars at Kaye's cheered at this; they all swore that Kaye made some of the best pies in Albion.

"And first place and the blue ribbon of the Portsmouth County Fair to—"

The judge paused, wanting to hold the crowd to himself for one more moment.

"—to Miss Edith Cottrell."

To loud and long applause, Miss Cottrell, cane in hand, climbed the steps onto the platform. She took the ribbon and pinned it to her sweater while the judge held the pie high in the air for her. "An old family recipe," she said. "An old Cottrell family recipe." She looked down at her blue ribbon, glowing.

You never would have known that Grandma was disappointed. She stood there, clapping her hands, for all the world as happy as a lark. But when Miss Cottrell came down the stairs and they announced the chocolate pie category, Grandma seemed to sag.

"I didn't even place," she said. "I knew that there would be too much nutmeg and cinnamon. They just clashed too much. I didn't even place."

"Mrs. Emerson, a judge who's just tasted seventy-five pies can't tell the difference after a while," Will said. "You know you make great pies."

Grandma smiled at him. "Well," she said, "I guess the people I care about like them well enough. I suppose I can settle for that."

"It's more than settling," said Will. "You make a pie for

someone, that's a way to tell them you love them. When Ma makes pies for us, it's her way of telling that she loves us. It doesn't matter that they aren't very good. Cole here has the advantage of not only getting the same message but getting it in something that tastes good."

"Your mother makes the best chocolate pie in Albion, Will Hurd, and you know it."

"My mother makes the only chocolate pie in Albion."

Grandpa found us then. He'd washed off everything that could get washed off with a hose, so now he was dirty and wet. He took one look at Grandma and knew he shouldn't ask about the pies. "Olivia," he said, "you know what you've been waiting for behind the barn?"

"You old fool. You didn't go ahead and do that?"

"We'll see you later, boys. Cole, you be back at the pickup by sunset. Will, Peter, we'll drop you off on the way home if you want." Grandpa took Grandma's hand and they headed off down the midway, towards the exhibition hall.

Grandpa could be cantankerous as all get-out, but when it came to Grandma, he smoothed out like an old dog circling down by a woodstove.

It was late afternoon by now, the sun starting to paint the tents a dark orange. All over the fair handlers were feeding the animals, and the sounds of eager goats and cows and pigs and horses filled the air. The canned music of the hawkers had turned off for a quick suppertime before the evening crowds came in, when everything would be lit up and noisy once more. For now the fair settled into a stillness, napping and gathering its energies after a long day's work.

107

Will had stayed in the Big Top to pick up his mother's chocolate pie ribbon. Peter went off to buy two stuffed cows for his sisters. And I walked slowly down the midway, stopping at some of the stalls I had already seen, until I got to the music stand, empty up to now. A slim woman as quiet and still as the hickory chair she sat on was tuning up a fiddle. Her long, mousy hair hid her face, keeping guard over her eyes. It faded into her long brown dress, draped right to her ankles, so she seemed out of place up there on that stand, so quiet, so still in a fair full of color and motion and shouting.

She picked up her fiddle slow, and ran the bow gently, softly over the strings to see if the music was in them. Then suddenly she cocked her elbow and jabbed the bow into the air, sending the music out as quick and fast as a prancing pony. The music was so happy your feet started to step in time, your hands slapped against the sides of your legs, and your soul couldn't help but dance to the rhythm.

And as the light faded, this happy music played, crowds gathering and then moving on, the music jumping and leaping like a thing alive, the woman hardly moving except for one foot keeping time, the fingers of her left hand running up and down the strings all in a frenzy, and the cocked arm shooting back and forth, back and forth, up and down, for all the world like she was sawing through the fiddle. And still the happy rain of that music sprinkled out all over.

I don't know how long she kept on. But I stood there and when she finished, dusk had stretched down the paths of the fair so that there was more light high up in the sky

108

than here below. She set her fiddle down, her face just hinting of a smile. As the crowd headed to the parking lot, she came to the edge of the stand, looking at me.

"You were my most faithful listener. I think I could play something just for you."

"Yes," I said, "I'd like that."

She hinted at a smile again, and then looked at me, I guess figuring what song would work just right. She sat down on the edge of the stand, adjusted her dress, and set the fiddle up to her chin. And then she played a song I had heard before. It was the song that Kaye had sung in church, and the long, shuddering strokes of her playing made me glad that the light had turned.

She played only to me. A few people stopped for a moment, but they went on; they could tell that this was something private. First she played on one string, keeping each note pure and separate, moving through the song lullaby-simple. Then she added another string, two singers falling to their knees together with their faces to the rising sun, one string humming to the other in a kind of melancholy way. The third time through, she ran all around the notes, playing with the melody like the sadness was all part of being happy, like they were one and the same thing.

Then she stopped, holding the last chord out long into the dusk.

"How did you know?" I asked, after a time.

"Ghost guessed," she said, hinting at her smile one more time. Then she went to put her fiddle away.

I met Will and Peter in front of the pickup, Will holding Mrs. Hurd's blue ribbon, and Peter with his two stuffed cows. I thought Grandpa would fuss because I was so late, but instead he had a big grin across his face. "Look, boy," he called, holding up a blue ribbon, bigger than any I had seen yet, tinged all around with gold. "Best in Show."

"Best what?"

"Best pie, of course. Best pie out of all the categories. Better even than Edith Cottrell's." Grandma sat in the pickup, holding back her smile, trying not to show too much how pleased she was.

"Miss Cottrell brought it to us," said Will. "We left the Big Top too early."

Then, from the back of the pickup, *maa, maa.* I walked around; up in the pickup bed Grandpa had tethered two goats, bleating in the cooling air. I hefted myself in and rubbed them between the horns.

"We can use them to keep down the brush behind the barn," he said to us, but we all knew he got them for more than that.

"They'll be pets before Christmas," Grandma called out the side window.

"Olivia, that isn't so."

Grandma just nodded. "I suppose you have names for them already?"

A long smile spread across Grandpa's face.

"You going to tell us?"

"Well," said Grandpa slowly, dragging it out. "Well, just in case these two goats tend to clash, I expect we should call them Nutmeg and Cinnamon."

Grandma smacked him on the top of his head, squashing his damp hat flat as we drove out of the fairgrounds.

SEVEN

IT WAS ALMOST DARK when we got home, the sun's last light reddening Cobb's Hill like war. The lamp in the hired man's room was low, but from behind the barn came the sound of wood splitting. We all three stood silent for a moment, out of the pickup, listening.

"Go talk to him," Grandma whispered to me.

Grandpa nodded. "Go ahead, boy. I'll tend to the goats." They watched me turn the corner of the barn. I walked slowly, unsurely. It seemed as if Dad had dropped away from my life like bait plucked cleanly off a hook.

There were still moments when something would happen and I would think about how I could tell Ma about it, and for a second, and sometimes even longer, it was as if she were still alive and I really could. Then she would die again.

But with Dad, even those moments did not come. There was hardly anything I needed to tell him. Yet he was still here.

He stood by a stump behind the house, hatchet in hand, chopping pine kindling. He had been in the hired man's room so long that the sun had faded from his skin, and his hands, flashing up and down, were the color of lard. He looked old, so old that I wondered if the hatchet would be

111

too heavy for him to heft into the air. But again and again it went up, parted the air beneath it, and took into the wood, ripping off a slice as neatly as a bloom peeling away its petals. The satisfying thwack of the hatchet as it hit the pine, the thud of it laying into the stump, made me want something I did not even know.

"I'll spell you," I called to his back.

He did not turn around. "No need. I'm fine."

I went over to the stump and bent down to pick up the kindling that lay around his feet. The smell of sap hung lightly in the air.

"Best to leave that be," he said. "I don't want to worry about hitting you." I stepped back.

Thwack. Thud.

"The fair was good."

He nodded. This piece had a knot in it that curled the grain, and he turned it around, looking for the best angle.

"We saw Coach DuChenney hit the bell on the slammer hammer."

Satisfied with the angle, he split off three quick pieces. They fell around his feet and into the pile. He bent down to pick up the next piece.

"Do you ever get angry at her?"

I don't know where the question came from. We had hardly talked about Ma since we came to Albion. We hesitated on the boundaries of her life like it was a hostile country.

Now, he stood bent over the stump, hatchet held down, and it suddenly came to me that he looked like Coach DuChenney, holding the mallet dug into the ground, six inches away from the slammer. Inside, Grandma turned the kitchen light on, and it shone across the yard, striking the stump but leaving him in shadow.

"There's no one left to be angry at," he whispered. "Not your mother. Not God. Not anyone."

"I get angry at her. Sometimes."

"Then at least you have something to hold on to."

It was almost too dark to split anymore; he had to use feel more than sight. The chops came shorter, and sometimes he had to wrench the hatchet through the wood to peel the pieces off.

"It doesn't have to be like this," I said. I took a deep breath. "Ma wouldn't want things like this."

"She's not here to see."

"I'm here. Grandma and Grandpa are here."

"A whole cloud of witnesses," he said, nodding his head. "Only thing is, there's nothing left to witness." He pointed with the hatchet to the graveyard. "The only ones who know anything are all out there and they're cold. And they're not saying anything."

Thwack. Thud.

"Then you may as well be out there with them, for all the good you're doing."

He stopped splitting and turned around for the first time and looked at me. His eyes were blank. "Someday I will be, and then I'll know." He turned back to the stump.

I left him there, the cold gathering around him like stone, chopping wood in the dark. He didn't come in for supper, and when I went to bed that night, the sound of splitting wood still filled the air. I read *The House at Pooh Corner* to its rhythm.

Grandpa, Grandma, and I drove to church the next

113

morning in deep silence, each knowing that the other was thinking of Dad but not sure what to say. Or if there was anything at all to say. They brightened up when we got to the service and Grandpa settled into the pew, ready to begin the List of Theological Errors. Grandma had tucked her "Best in Show" blue ribbon between the pages of her Bible, and she fidgeted some while Pastor Hurd preached on the deadly sin of pride, but it wasn't enough to keep her from showing the ribbon to Mrs. Dowdle after the service. "Olivia, I've never seen anything like it," she said, fingering the gold. And bless her heart, Miss Cottrell came up to Grandma and put her arms around her.

The sky had crept low over the church by the time we got out, big-bellied clouds so close that you could just about reach up and prick them to let out their snow. And before we got home, someone had. It started with just a few flakes in the air, so few that you couldn't be sure if they were really there. Then they started to fall together, lines of them driven out of the northeast by a ringing wind. And then the lines turned to sheets, and then the sheets to one billowing storm, until by the time we got to the farm Grandpa was driving with his head out of the side window so that he wouldn't miss the road.

It snowed all that day, a snow so thick and gray that it turned the afternoon to deep dusk. There was no difference between the sky and the land; it was all snow rushing down and then shooting up alongside the house. The wind whisked it against the windowpanes, at times softly, at times like pebbles when the snow turned icy. All the world around us filled and filled, and when Grandpa and I went out to check on The Frisian, the cows, and Cinnamon and

114

Nutmeg, the landscape was as new as if I had never set foot on the farm.

Night, and still the snow came down. I finished the chapter on the origins of the Civil War that Mr. Shaw had assigned for a test, but I knew that there would be no school tomorrow.

That evening, I sat with Grandpa and Grandma in the living room, the woodstove shedding heat to bar the cold, all the lights lit to push back the dark. Grandma had rolled old hooked rugs and tucked them under the doors to keep out the draft and set a pot of cider to hotten up on the stove. "We look like a scene from 'Snow Bound,'" Grandma said.

"That's a poem from Whittier," Grandpa said to me, "the same one who wrote 'Barefoot Girl.'"

Grandma didn't answer him. She stirred the cider with a long cinnamon stick and began to recite.

> "What matter how the night behaved?
> What matter how the north-wind raved?
> Blow high, blow low, not all its snow
> Could quench our hearth-fire's ruddy glow."

She poured out the cider in old chipped mugs, and we sipped it quietly, listening to the snow against the windows, the smells of the cinnamon and cider mingling with that of the stove's hot iron.

"Cole," said Grandpa suddenly, "did we ever tell you about the time old Grandad Erastus rode the ice down Cobb's Hill out here?" He started to laugh and didn't wait for me to answer; he wanted to tell the story.

"Old Erastus, he'd been out part of the night rolling the

115

roads after a storm, dragging a roller to flatten the snow for the sleighs the next day. But the snow was so thick he decided he'd wait until morning to finish up. It wasn't as easy a decision as it is for some people, that being a Sunday and him being a deacon scheduled to read the Scriptures and deliver the long prayer. But he set out before dawn and finished before anyone else was up.

"Old Erastus, when he stood on top of the hill out front and saw the new sun shining on it, he couldn't help but want to slide on down it. He went and got a barrel stave, still figuring that no one was out, and pushed off. Pretty soon he started to pick up more speed than he wanted, and he tried to dig his heels in, like this. But the hill was icy and slick, and all he did was to turn himself around so that he was heading backwards. He reached a hand out to try and get himself right, but he was going so fast now that his glove just tore off. He tried pulling up on the barrel stave, but that just set him spinning like a top.

"By the time he hit bottom he was going faster than he ever had in his life, and what with the spinning and the speed, he flipped over and his leg went out and caught a pine. Broke it clean. The leg, not the pine.

"Old Erastus, he isn't going to tell a single soul what he's been doing. He takes that barrel stave and limps on home. He gets through breakfast and drives on out to church without saying a thing. He stands up there and reads the passage and gives the long prayer. It isn't until after he gets home that he sends one of his boys for the doctor.

"'How'd this happen?' the doctor asks when he goes there.

116

"Erastus leans forward"—and here Grandpa leaned out at me like he was Erastus himself—"and he says real slow, 'Doctor, isn't there a single thing a man can do in private in this town?'"

Grandpa sat back and laughed until the echo filled the room. Grandma put down the mug of cider she'd been blowing on and looked for all the world like she was remembering what had happened in this very room more than a century ago. Maybe, in a way, she was.

It came to me that the story wasn't just a story to Grandpa. It was his own history, coming down to him from generation to generation, a story about people whose blood we carried. For a moment there was no difference between Grandpa and Erastus; I felt the story settle down into me until it was more memory than story.

And still the snow came down.

For two more days the storm didn't let up, but set to against the house for all it was worth. Grandpa kept the woodstove running hot and Grandma played hymns loud on the phonograph at night to quiet the wind. They called Miss Cottrell and Mrs. Dowdle to check on them. Fine, they said, but they hadn't seen the likes of this storm since 1934, when the whole town shut down and Albion Grace Church of the Holy Open Bible had missed its morning service. Never happened since.

It was the storm that finally sent me up to the attic, holding a flashlight and wearing two sweaters. Some fine snow had sifted in past the windowsills and the air was still and chilled. Crouching low—the ceiling was only shoulder high—I dragged a box away from the window and brushed off the snow.

117

Shadows lay over everything, thrown by the bare light-bulb to settle into the dust. Christmas was stored up here in a stack of boxes; a string of Christmas lights tried to escape from one. A set of Lionel trains lay stored in perfect boxes in an old bookcase, hidden by two Windsor chairs piled on top of each other, their legs gnawed thin by some dog gone for a generation or two. An iron-cornered trunk hunkered down in one corner, empty but for cedar shavings and a beaver hat in the bottom. Nothing ever changed up here; it had been the same since the first year I had come.

The flashlight beam poked into the corners: an old Bible glittering with gold, a stack of school readers, a set of encyclopedias too old to use but too expensive to throw out, a collection of Joseph Lincoln novels. I could see my breath frosted in the air, and I pulled one of the sweaters over my mouth and nose and breathed in the warm, wet, wooly air. The books I'd looked through before. The readers had the name Erastus Emerson written boldly across their title pages, flourishes drawn under the *E*'s. Grandpa had collected the Joseph Lincoln books and printed his name carefully on the back covers, along with the dates.

So I grabbed the Bible instead, untying the ribbon that held it together and folding back the heavy cover. Coming out of its long rest, the spine creaked and let go a flake or two. Gold tipped all the pages, still shining when I blew the dust away and shone the light full on it.

Hieronymous Emerson on the red-lettered title page. *Christmas Day, 1844.* A piece of tissue separated the page for an etching of Christ in Gethsemane, and on the tissue, a faded message written in long, slanted letters:

For my beloved husband, on our first Christmas together, from your loving wife, Lydia. Every letter written on that delicate paper was as perfect as if it had been ruled.

Family Records followed the title page. First the record of marriage: Hieronymous Emerson to Lydia Adams, December 22, 1844. Red and gold decoration fluttered around the names, and ribbons of yellow roses filled each margin. The next pages held lots of births, marriages, and deaths, all names I had heard before. Even Hieronymous's death was marked by those same slanted letters: *He has laid down his humanity, that one thing that for a time has made him a little lower than the angels. February 1, 1898.* All the names were in order, the dates following, all in the script on the title page.

Except for the record of births, where the names seemed out of order. First came Brewster James Emerson, October 8, 1845, then Grace Anne Emerson, born April 14, 1847, and then Stephen David Emerson, March 9, 1850. Hannah Kathleen Emerson came much later, April 6, 1858, and then Sophie Rebecca Emerson, July 25, 1860, and Betsy Margaret Emerson, April l, 1862. But after Betsy, somehow Erastus Cottrell Emerson snuck in on January 2, 1859. But stranger still, a dark line crossed through *Cottrell,* and *Emerson* was written with a heavy, awkward hand, not like any of the other names printed in the Bible.

I switched off the flashlight and carried the book downstairs out of the cold. Behind me, the snow still sifted past the sill.

"I haven't seen that for years," Grandma said when I brought the Bible into the kitchen. The smell of hot chocolate filled the room, and I cupped the mug in my hands to warm them.

"It's probably been up in the attic for a while."

"When I was just a bride in this house it was on a table in the best room. But then Great-grandma was so sick and we made that room into a sickroom so we'd be close. I guess we never brought the Bible back down."

I opened the record of births. "Do you know why part of Erastus's name is crossed out?"

Grandma peered at the page and ran her finger across the name. "From what I remember, he was adopted."

"So he was a Cottrell first?"

Grandma nodded her head. "Lots of families after the war adopted nieces and nephews. So many of the fathers were killed, someone had to take them in. So mothers made choices, sending their children to this uncle or that aunt. Most families were glad of the extra hand."

"But the Cottrells weren't related to the Emersons."

"No."

"So why would Hieronymous adopt Erastus?"

Grandma took a long sip of her hot chocolate.

"I couldn't tell you that. Maybe there just wasn't any-one else who could take him in."

Suddenly, Erastus, the deacon who slid down icy hills on barrel staves, changed. I imagined his mother, wearing black, taking her little boy by the hand and, face set hard against the tears, handing him over to a family of strangers and turning away. And he would have watched her go out the gate and down the hill, her back to him, as he stood in the doorway of a strange house. And Hieronymous would have been glad to get him because he'd be an extra hand.

120

And as I imagined the scene, suddenly another image joined it—the Sin Eater, standing by a tree looking down and watching the black-dressed mother walking firmly away.

Grandma put the Bible back in the best parlor again, on the same table where it had been when she first saw it. "It's good to keep some things the same," she said, giving it a brisk dusting. I wondered what the Sin Eater would have said to that.

On the fourth day the snow slacked off, so by late afternoon the sun burned dim holes through the gray. On Thursday it came up in a blue sky, so bright against the white I had to shield my eyes on the way to school. Grandpa drove me down, the rear wheels of the pickup skidding back and forth on the unplowed roads. In town, everyone seemed to be out shoveling their front walks, heaving the snow into jagged heaps. A plow had been through the school parking lot, and Coach DuChenney, red-faced and jetting steamy breath into the air, was shoveling what the plow had left away from the gym doors. I wished later that I had stopped to help.

You'd think that Mr. Shaw would have given us a day to get into the habit of school again, but when we came into class for first period, the exams were laid across our desks, an array of multiple choice and fill-in and true/false that took up eight pages. Eight. Just for the origins of the Civil War. Imagine if we had gotten to a battle.

"Attached to the back of your exams," he announced, "you'll find your local history assignment. We'll be studying the ways in which the Civil War affected Albion, and you each have a different topic to research. But before you get to that, you have other things to worry about." He was right.

I never made it to page eight and turned in the test hoping that Mr. Shaw knew the difference between law and grace.

Will was already dressed and shooting baskets by the time I got to the gym. "Hurry up," he called. So I did. Coach DuChenney had been true to his word. A cart filled with basketballs stood by the locker room, and by the time I got out, most of them were bouncing across the floor and arching against backboards. It was a beautiful sound.

We weren't three minutes into the period before we were shirts and skins, playing half-court.

We weren't ten minutes into the period before we were all wondering where Coach DuChenney was. It started with cautious looks between passes, watching for the office door to slam open. Then the play started to slow, and finally it was only Ian, palming the ball and taking one last shot.

Will walked over to the door and knocked, but there was no answer. "Coach," he hollered through the glass. "Coach."

Ian tossed the ball to me and we went to the door. Will turned the knob slowly. "Coach?" He peered in, then swung the door open.

Coach DuChenney stared out at us, his face white and wet, his right hand fiercely grasping his left arm. Then his wild eyes closed, he groaned, and he twisted and fell, the back of his head thudding onto the tile floor and throwing blood up over Ian's chest. Will sprinted down the hall towards the office, but Ian cupped his hands gently, gently under Coach's head, blood seeping onto his fingers through thinning hair. We all crowded in, eager to see.

Coach opened his eyes and looked up and saw Ian Waleski. He wet his lips and spoke slowly, in a graveled voice. "Say a prayer for me."

Ian nodded. "I'll say it."

Then Coach closed his eyes again, and suddenly my eyes blurred with tears.

I had seen death before. One minute Coach was there, bleeding and lying on the floor, and breathing. And then he wasn't there. And it wasn't just because he wasn't breathing anymore. It was as if that body had nothing more to do with Coach DuChenney. Somehow it had become unimportant.

Ian kept his hands under the coach until the sirens came and paramedics rushed in and shoved him aside. Lights and stretchers and tanks with long tubes filled the office. A siren screeched, and Mrs. Pluckett came in and hustled us to the other side of the gym.

I pushed through the doors and stood out in the space Coach had cleared of snow, the sweat freezing on me. I stood there remembering until Will found me and dragged me back inside.

Coach was buried three days later, on a cloudy gray day threatening snow. Peter, Will, and I stood together near an old priest; an air force jacket covered his robes. Beside him stood Ian, dressed in a short robe, chanting the prayer.

"To Paradise may the angels bring you,
And may the martyrs come to meet you on your way,
And may you be led into the holy city, Jerusalem.
All the choirs of angels make you welcome there,
And with Lazarus once so ill and poor,
May peaceful joy be now forever yours. Amen."

"Amen," whispered Peter afterwards.

"Amen," Will and I said together.

The cold numbed our feet, and even the priest leaned from one side to the other, using his weight to warm his toes. We stayed until the attendants started to shovel the soil over the casket—a familiar sound—then Grandpa drove us back to school for the afternoon.

Mrs. Pluckett canceled the school Halloween party; it wasn't seemly, she said, to hold a celebration so soon after Coach's death. It was just as well. Halloween night a freezing rain slicked down all the sidewalks and roads enough to satisfy old Erastus himself with his barrel stave. With the rain peltering down, no one could go out, so Pastor Hurd opened up the basement of Albion Grace Church of the Holy Open Bible for all the elementary-school kids. There wasn't much candy but Mrs. Hurd brought out a batch of chocolate pies, Will and Peter ran the relays, the kids fumbling or dashing depending on their costumes, and Pastor Hurd read a story about the monster that came out at night with all the church lights turned off. Peter's sisters loved it.

I didn't get down to the church because of the ice on Cobb's Hill, but Peter said later that it would have been worth coming just to hear the story. Will said it would have

124

been worth coming just to help them empty the freezer of chocolate pies.

Thanksgiving was quiet too that year, maybe because Coach's death still hung around the school. You couldn't pass the gym without thinking about it. The sky seemed to agree; it stayed cloudy and low, so the paper turkeys and Pilgrim hats that adorned the school windows looked shabby. Down past the Commons, Kaye had decorated the front of her diner with cornstalks from Mr. Cooper's field, and across the way Mr. Lanier had a cardboard Pilgrim standing by the snowblower in his window. (After Halloween he put the bright red rototiller away and dragged out the bright green snowblower.) Things seemed halfhearted.

But Grandma wouldn't let things go that way forever. By early morning of Thanksgiving Day, the house smelled of roasting turkey, mince pie, stuffing, creamed onions, and popovers, brown and doughy. Grandma ran from the oven to baste, to the dining room to straighten the table-cloth, to the stove to stir the onions, to the kitchen table to spread cinnamon on the cooling pies, to the china cabinet to take out the good glassware, and to the living room to remind Grandpa that it was time to fetch Miss Cottrell and Mrs. Dowdle.

"Now?"

"Yes," said Grandma.

"You going to wipe that flour out of your hair?"

"No. I'm going to leave it there."

"Makes you look older."

Grandma ran her hands over her apron, walked over to Grandpa, and rubbed them across his head. "Now we're a pair."

125

He leapt out of his seat and ran after her, and she ran down the hall, laughing almost to a squeal. I could see that Miss Cottrell and Mrs. Dowdle would have to wait.

Miss Cottrell was fussing some when she came through the kitchen door, and she pointed out through dinner that the turkey was a little drier than it needed to have been if they had sat down to the table on time. She was wearing a cornered hat pinned securely to her hair, its three pheasant feathers waving behind her with every toss of her head. I heard Grandpa whisper to Grandma that she'd best not be abroad during the season, and Grandma reached and slapped his knee. Miss Cottrell suggested that the onions were on the overdone side as well.

Mrs. Dowdle had spent the morning talking on the phone to her three sons, three daughters-in-law, and seven grandchildren. I could see she was thinking about them, because suddenly she would break into a big smile for no reason at all, and then the next moment her eyes would tear up, and then she'd be back to smiling again. "Every Thanksgiving makes us remember so many other Thanksgivings," she said.

"I'm not sure I see why it should," said Miss Cottrell. She was a little pouty.

"But it does," said Grandma. "They all seem to melt into each other, don't they? It's as if we were celebrating them all at the same time."

I didn't tell Grandma that I was doing the best I could to think about only this one. I didn't trust myself to think about any of the others—the lonesome ones of the past two years, or the warm, stuffed ones of earlier.

Grandpa passed the turkey around one more time and

offered some to Miss Cottrell, who shook her feathers.

"Where's your father?" she asked me suddenly.

I looked up, startled. It had been so long since he'd eaten with us that we had just begun to take it for granted.

"He's upstairs," I answered. "In the hired man's room."

"Is he sick? He should be eating Thanksgiving dinner if he's not sick."

"He'll be down later," said Grandma.

"I see," said Miss Cottrell, putting her fork deliberately on the table.

Grandma began clearing the plates, Mrs. Dowdle helping. Grandpa wondered if we should feed The Frisian some extra grain on this Thanksgiving, and added that we wanted to be sure to take some leftover pie to Nutmeg and Cinnamon. Miss Cottrell's feathers waved at this, but she didn't say anything. Grandpa finished a long draft of cider.

"Getting about time to paint that wrought iron again, Miss Cottrell?" Grandpa asked.

She nodded. "Almost past time, Hiram. You haven't painted that fence in four years."

"Three. But we'll let the winter go, then get to it come spring. With young Cole here to help it won't take long."

Silence. Long silence. It was becoming the kind of meal where people kept running out of things to say.

Grandma and Mrs. Dowdle came back in, carrying pies. "Mince and wild blueberry," said Mrs. Dowdle. "Such a choice to have to make."

"No apple," observed Grandpa.

Grandma kicked him under the table and set to cutting the pies.

"Oh, Cole," said Mrs. Dowdle, "before I forget, I've

127

brought you something." She reached into the carpet-bag purse she'd hung from the chairback and handed me a small package wrapped in tissue. Its edges were sharp and tore through the tissue as I opened it—the tintype of the Sin Eater. His eyes stared out at me, and I must have looked surprised.

"You stared at it so long the last time you were in my house, I thought you might like to have it."

"I would. Thank you."

"It's been in the family forever. My grandmother's grandmother had it."

"Then maybe it should stay in your family."

"No," she smiled. "This should stay here in New Hampshire, not in Patagonia or Polynesia or wherever my children all end up. It's got a New England soul, just like you."

"But the Sin Eater," I said, "he wasn't from here."

"No," answered Mrs. Dowdle. "Even in that tintype you can tell he looks a little bit out of place."

"Do you know where he died?"

"I think he died in a fire up at his farm, before his family came over. But the wildest stories grew up about him afterwards."

"So you don't believe the cows knelt to him," said Grandpa.

Miss Cottrell sniffed abruptly.

"Well," said Mrs. Dowdle slowly, "if they didn't they should have. If it hadn't been for him, the only ones sitting at this table would be Miss Cottrell and you, Olivia."

"That's right," nodded Grandpa. "The fever would have put an end to the Emersons and Dowdles both."

I had never heard this story, and it didn't take much to get Mrs. Dowdle telling it.

"After the Sin Eater came, there were lots of stories around town about him. Most people just stayed away from him, and he seemed to like it that way. But my great-grandfather and Hiram's here, they used to hunt on past his farm, and it got so that they would help him out with chores come fall, and he would help them out in the spring.

"One wet April the fever came, and there was nothing the doctor in town could do. Whole families just got wiped out, and there didn't seem to be any medicine that would help. Then one Sunday, every one of the Dowdle children and every one of the Emerson children came down with it, all together, like it had somehow snuck in during the night. The doctor had told everyone in town that when someone came down with a fever, they were to be put in the smallest room in the house that had a fireplace. The fire should be blazing, and they should be under as many quilts as they could stand. No food, and only a little bit of water. So there were all these children under mounds of quilts, the fever taking them.

"It was the next day that the Sin Eater came to the Dowdle house, ready to help out with the spring chores. He took one look at those sweltering children and ripped off all the quilts but one. He threw water over the fire and opened every window in the house so that the wind could blow through. Then with his own hands he made up broth and fed it to all the children, as tender as a mother.

"Then he went on to the Emerson house and did the same thing.

129

"He came to those houses every day for the next two weeks, bringing down soups that he had learned about back in his home country. Our great-grandparents, they did everything he told them to do: changing the sheets, keeping the windows open, pouring broth down those children like there was no tomorrow.

"That spring, more than half the children of Albion died. Half. Of the rest, many never grew up right. The fever left them weak. But there wasn't a single Emerson or Dowdle child that died. Not one. And that's why I have the old tintype, Cole. My great-grandpa had it taken and they kept it in the parlor."

"Is that why he's buried in the Emerson graveyard?" I asked.

"I'd forgotten that," said Grandpa. "But that's right. Hieronymous buried him there."

"I'll try another piece of that mince pie now, Olivia," said Miss Cottrell.

We were quiet after that, and I thought about the Sin Eater, alone in his farmhouse, waiting for his family. I wondered if this doctoring was the one thing he had written about in the letter that the Gealys had. And I thought about Hieronymous burying him in the Emerson Burial Yard, not far from the two blank stones, but far enough away to still be alone.

That night, Grandpa and I drove Miss Cottrell and Mrs. Dowdle home, Grandpa whistling the first Christmas carols of the season. The roads were deserted, so on the way home Grandpa let me drive the pickup, the first time I'd driven on something that wasn't a meadow. When I got back to my bedroom, I propped the tintype up on the mantel, beside *The House at Pooh Corner.*

I felt the season passing and winter coming on. The year was wheeling past like the fair's Ferris wheel. And me? I was fumbling into stories I would someday tell.

And so we came to deep winter and the longest Christmas.

EIGHT

Miss COTTRELL ran the Christmas decoration of Albion Grace Church of the Holy Open Bible as she imagined her ancestor, Colonel Franklin Cottrell, ran the 21st New Hampshire in its Civil War battles. Actually he only led his men into one battle, but it was enough to make him a hero in Albion. An oval-framed picture of the colonel ruled over the lobby of the Albion Town Hall; he stared out with blazing, wide-open eyes, sword hilt in one hand, captured Confederate flag in the other, looking for all the world as if he were posing for Mount Rushmore.

Grandpa said he had won his one battle only because he'd been born in New Hampshire, where east and west aren't as important as up and down. During the retreat from Antietam, he'd been commanded to take his company east along the river to reconnoiter. He ordered his

New Hampshirers west instead, ignoring the advice of lieutenants and compasses. ("A real Cottrell," Grandpa added at this point.) But by chance he came up behind six squadrons of Confederate soldiers, whom he captured— the only Union victory in that battle. He came back to New Hampshire to parades. His grave marker is the biggest in the churchyard, and every Memorial Day Miss Cottrell decorates it with a Union flag across the stone and a Confederate flag on the ground beneath it.

Come Christmas, the church counted on her to be just as consistent with the decorations. Under each long window along the aisles boughs of evergreen sprayed out, a long yellow-white beeswax candle coming through their middle, the whole tied together with red and green satin ribbons that draped almost to the floor. Over the back entry hung a bright banner made to look like stained glass. Under silhouettes of the Holy Family and the ox and the donkey, Miss Cottrell had sewn a poem in bright gold shimmering letters.

> *Hand by hand*
> *We shall us take,*
> *And joy and bliss*
> *Shall we make.*
> *For the devil of hell*
> *Man does forsake,*
> *And God's Son*
> *Is maked our mate.*

It was, she explained, a medieval poem, Catholic to be sure, but not inappropriate on Christmas Day. Pastor Hurd let it stand, he said, because it was traditional.

132

(Grandpa said he let it stand because he was afraid of Miss Cottrell.)

Red and green satin ribbons wreathed the end of each pew, getting wider and wider as the pews got closer to the front; for the last three pews a gold ribbon ran in and out between the red and green satin. Around the pulpit, a single gold ribbon. Beneath it, a manger filled with golden straw and surrounded by banks of red and white poinsettias, blooming for all they were worth.

Most everyone complained about Miss Cottrell's military tactics; she approached decoration time as though she were about to lay siege to the church. She never asked for volunteers. She assigned church members to companies, each with its orders, requisitioned supplies, and sector of the church. She fixed the gold ribbon to the pulpit herself, but other than that she used her cane to point, give directions, and sometimes smack a soldier who didn't quite get things right.

"A battle can be lost with a single small detail," she said. "Do it again."

All through December the church grumbled. "Too much work." "Always the same." "That Miss Cottrell."

But that Miss Cottrell pretended she couldn't hear the grumbles, and by Christmas Eve it no longer mattered. Except for the last two, we had spent every Christmas Eve in Albion Grace Church of the Holy Open Bible, arriving through soft snow an hour before midnight, singing carols to welcome in the day as the candles glowed against the frosty windows. At midnight, we sang "Silent Night" as if we were all surprised that this thing had come yet again. And maybe we all were.

No one grumbled then. The sweet honey smell of the beeswax candles mixed with the evergreen boughs and filled the church like incense. The quiet singing, the feel of us crowded together in the pews, the familiar repetition made the night magical. And when we came out of the warm church, the clear, cold air stung our cheeks into cherries. We drove home—once The Frisian pulled us home on a sled as we huddled warm under scratchy wool blankets—and I trudged, already asleep, on up to bed, half wondering if the best part of Christmas wasn't already over.

Decorating the house was another matter. Grandpa fussed and muttered about it, remembering the days when everyone in Albion would go to the church on Christmas Eve to exchange presents. "We didn't bother to decorate the houses then," he said. "We were too busy just farming to do that sort of thing."

"Well you're not too busy now," Grandma reminded him, and sent him out to the south woods to fetch the spruce he'd marked earlier in the summer.

We cut it down together that year, the first time I'd done it with him. It was a nine-footer if it was an inch, perfect around, more blue than green and prickly with the winter cold. We twined up all of its branches and carted it back on a toboggan, our boots breaking through a layer of glistening ice left by a storm the night before, but the toboggan sliding around as if it were Erastus himself we were carrying, sliding down his wild hill.

We set the tree in its stand two weeks before Christmas, and while the phonograph played carols, Grandma arranged boughs she'd clipped over the fireplace and across the tops of the bookcases. She ran a red-and-white ribbon through them and nestled gold and silver balls where there seemed a space. Then, over the mantel, she hung an evergreen wreath, the boughs so fresh that sap ran out their ends in the warm room. When it was up, she sprinkled it with mica dust, so that it sparkled no matter where I was in the room. Everything smelled of the woods.

The tree we wouldn't decorate until after the service Christmas Eve, but until Christmas there was something to do each night. One night there were the small hurricane lamps to put in each window, laden with scented kerosene Grandma bought special from Roy Lanier's Hardware. Another night there were the colored lights to sort and test. And for three nights we had popcorn and cranberries to string; Grandma pushed the popcorn through the needle like she was sewing a quilt, which she could do almost without looking. But Grandpa and I always had bloody thumbs by the time we were finished.

And then there was the night for the crèche scene.

Grandma kept the figures wrapped in tissue in their rock maple stable that Grandpa's father had made back in 1893; the date was burned into the bottom. The Holy Family, the ox and donkey, and the shepherds were carved out of soft pine and painted brown and yellow, so that they would seem at home in the straw. After a year in the attic, most of them would need to be touched up a bit, and whenever we had been there to celebrate Christmas with Grandpa and Grandma, this was Dad's job. "A steady hand," said Grandma. "It needs a steady hand."

Ten days before Christmas, Grandma spread newspaper across the kitchen table and set the figures on top. "Call your father, Cole," Grandma said. "See if he'll come and paint these up for us."

Dad hardly ever came down these days, not even to get warm. Grandma would bring him a tray at mealtime and leave the door from the kitchen open so that some heat could float up the stairs, but there was more of a cold draft that fell into the house below than warm breezes that went up. He hardly spoke with us anymore. And though I sometimes saw him watching me outside at chores or when I came home from school, he would only wave and back away from the window.

"Dad," I called up the stairs, knowing he wouldn't come and probably wouldn't answer. "Dad, we need you to paint the Holy Family." I went and sat down at the kitchen table. We all sat quietly for a long time.

The squeak of the door to the hired man's room opening. The sound of stairs taking weight. And Dad, cheeks and nose red, standing in the doorway, looking at us as though we were strangers.

"The paints and brushes are in the kitchen desk, top right," Grandma said, only half turning around. "You know."

Slowly Dad went over to the desk and opened the drawer. He took out the paints and a brush. He went over to the kitchen sink, wet the brush, and filled a Mason jar with water. Then he sat down at the table and picked up the baby Jesus.

"It's been a hard year for them, up in the attic," he said to no one.

I didn't know what to say. I had gotten so used to him

136

not being there that I couldn't think of anything to tell him.

He picked up the baby Jesus and began to paint the swaddling clothes white. He held the baby in the palm of his hand, steady. We watched him paint, Grandma and I, and when Grandpa came in to check on the woodstove, he sat down and watched too. In the living room the carols played right on.

We sat there for ten minutes, twenty minutes, forever, watching Dad paint. He used a washed-out yellow for the cow, and a dark brown for the donkey. For Mary he painted in a blue mantle with silver fringes, and a red smock underneath.

Joseph he lingered over a long time, then dipped his brush in black paint.

"Don't you think that Joseph deserves a matching color?" asked Grandma. The words felt large in the silent room.

Dad looked up at me, as if I had been the one who asked. Then he set the brush into the Mason jar. I could see the black paint swirl into the water.

"Let him be as he is," said Dad. "There wasn't much he did anyway." He slid his chair back, pushed himself up, crossed the kitchen, and went up the stairs as though he were very tired. We heard the door to the hired man's room close.

I went to the bottom of the stairs. "Goodnight," I called up. He didn't answer.

As we got closer to Christmas, Grandma got more frantic. There were all sorts of butter cookies to make. The Christmas cake was still to wrap and deliver. There was ribbon candy to stretch and she didn't have enough sugar and where was that flat pan that worked so well last year?

Mr. Shaw's first-period history class was getting frantic too. While everyone else, it seemed, was getting ready for a class party, we were spending our time researching Albion during the Civil War. "Finish the research before school lets out," Mr. Shaw said, "and you can write the report over break." Some break.

It was Will's idea to go partners, and when Mr. Shaw agreed, we decided to research my subject: Ephraim Cottrell and the Role of Substitutes. "C'mon," Will said. "We'll write on how you could pay someone to be your substitute in the Civil War, then on how Ephraim Cottrell decided to be this substitute and got killed for it."

The first part was easy to find out about. If you were drafted, you could pay three hundred dollars to have a substitute go for you—a lot of money in those days. But after that, we couldn't find much. Mrs. DuBois over in the Albion Free Public Library first suggested the newspaper archives, but those didn't start until 1870. Then she showed us a town history of Albion, but it didn't say anything about Ephraim Cottrell.

"Look for other things around the same time that could give you clues," she suggested. But the only entry in the history for 1862, when Ephraim died in the battle of Antietam, said that P. Clarke, N. Bowdoin, H. Emerson, and B. Boyd were elected selectmen, and that H. Emerson erected a third sawmill downstream from his first two above the Little Hosmer. Nothing about Ephraim Cottrell.

"You could have tried the town records over at the

courthouse," Mrs. DuBois said as she chewed thoughtfully at the end of her pencil, "but they were all destroyed when the courthouse burned down in the twenties. There would have been a record there of who paid to have Ephraim Cottrell substitute for him." She paused, considering. "You might try the church records. The church was one of the first buildings put up in Albion and usually the pastor kept the records himself. There might not be much, but you might at least find a record of Ephraim's birth, and whether he had children."

We headed for Albion Grace Church of the Holy Open Bible.

There's something about a church when it's empty and dark that makes it seem like it shouldn't be disturbed. When we closed the door behind us, the echo reverberated in the sanctuary. The late afternoon light stained the pews a strange yellow, and all the Christmas boughs seemed dark and dead. When Pastor Hurd walked up behind us, we startled at his voice.

"I didn't mean to scare you boys."

"You didn't," I lied.

"You did," Will overruled.

He only smiled and looked around. "A church without its people is a sad-looking building. It'll look different come Christmas Eve. But now, what are you two up to?"

"We need to look at the church records for 1862. We're trying to find out something about Ephraim Cottrell."

"The same one up on the Civil War plaque?"

"Yes."

"In my study. Far bookcase, lowest shelf. The records are marked by years." He looked at his watch. "I have to go downstairs. Miss Cottrell will be here any minute and I still haven't found all the white candles she's been asking for."

"She's a real general," said Will.

"Five star," said Pastor Hurd, saluting.

Pastor Hurd's study had the dry, musty smell of very old books—mostly because his walls were lined with them. Sets of leather-bound books marched sternly across the shelves, the gold faded and the leather turned to light orange. Three or four lay open on his desk, and when we moved them to make space, they left a powder of leather behind them that we blew onto the floor.

The records were in heavy ledgers, bound in black leather and smelling of age. The spines groaned and cracked when we opened them on the desk, and the yellow pages turned stiffly; it had been a long time since anyone had read these brown-inked words. Each year began with a list of births, marriages, deaths, and burials. Sometimes the minister added a short comment: *March 9, 1822. Birth of Eleazer Devotion. May his name be his life.* Or *April 6, 1824. Death of Abigail Proctor. In giving a child she went to be with her own Father. Burial April 8, 1824.* Lists of names and dates and forgotten stories marched up and down and across pages like shadows of things that once were.

We found Ephraim Cottrell in 1835, born on July 25. No comment by his name. He didn't appear again until 1853, when he married Charity Devotion, but then he appeared in the next three years, the first two under deaths.

140

February 3, 1854. Death of son of Ephraim and Charity Cottrell.

July 9, 1855. Death of daughter of Ephraim and Charity Cottrell.

January 2, 1859. Birth of Erastus Cottrell, son of Ephraim and Charity Cottrell.

There was a moment when something seemed familiar, and then I knew. This was the same date I had found in Grandpa's Bible. Here was the same Erastus who later became Erastus Emerson.

"Will, Ephraim's son is an ancestor of mine."

"Everyone in Albion is an ancestor of everyone else. Let's find his death."

We paged through three years until we came to 1862. His name was only a short way down the list of deaths.

September 27, 1862. Death of Ephraim Cottrell at Antietam.

The comment that followed was in a different hand, as though it had been added later.

Remains returned October 10, 1862. Buried October 12, 1862. Exhumed October 15, 1862.

And beneath that, another Cottrell entry.

October 13, 1862. Death of Charity Cottrell. Suicide. Not buried.

We looked at these entries a long time, read them over, and then looked at each other. "What went on here?" asked Will quietly.

"Why dig up a body and then bury it again?"

"And why wasn't Charity buried?"

Will hefted the book off the desk, holding it open to the page. "Let's go ask Dad."

We found him up in the attic on his hands and knees, Miss Cottrell standing behind him, pointing with her cane. "You might try that box there, young reverend."

"Miss Cottrell, it's marked Communion Cups."

"Things aren't always what they seem on the outside. Didn't they teach you that at your fancy seminary?"

Pastor Hurd sighed. He moved three smaller boxes and opened up the box Miss Cottrell had pointed to.

"Well?" she said.

"Hymnals."

"You see. Things aren't always what they seem. Let's try that one over there."

"Which one?"

"The one marked Hymnals."

Pastor Hurd wearily began lugging stacks of hymnals off this next box.

"Dad," said Will.

"Why does she always have to pick the box on the bottom?" he said under his breath.

"Pastor Hurd?" I said.

"He's busy," said Miss Cottrell. "This is a church matter."

"But Miss Cottrell," said Will, "this is about a suicide."

"A suicide?" said Pastor Hurd, setting down the stack of hymnals.

"And a missing body," I added.

"Perhaps I had better go see what these boys are talking

142

about, Miss Cottrell. If you want to keep looking, you might try that one."

She peered across the attic. "Which?"

"The one marked Candles." We went back downstairs and into Pastor Hurd's study.

"Set it here," he said, pointing to the desk, "and let's see." His voice was excited, as though he were about to come upon something important. Will pointed to the entries, and Pastor Hurd sat down to read them over. He must have read them four or five times. Then he said something that I had not expected.

"There's a lot of pain here, an awful lot."

"Can you tell what happened?" asked Will.

"I can guess at some of it. Ephraim Cottrell died on September 17, 1862. That was the bloodiest day of the battle of Antietam. By the time it was over, thousands of boys were dead. Thousands."

"How did they find Ephraim?"

"That's what's so interesting. How did they find him? All those bodies all over the field, across fencerows, in the streams. How did they find this one? And even if they found him, why bring him back to Albion?"

"Maybe he was put in a casket and shipped home," I said.

"But why? All those soldiers were buried right on the battlefield, most just where they had been killed. Some in mass graves. Why should this one be brought back when everyone else was buried right there?"

"Maybe someone arranged it," Will suggested. Pastor Hurd nodded, staring at the records as if they would suddenly speak.

"Yes, it's possible. If someone had connections with the army and had enough money to pay for shipping the body, and if he was in some political situation where he could call in a favor, maybe it could have been done.

"But now, back to these other two records. A month after the battle, the body comes back to Albion. Ephraim is buried in the churchyard. The next day his wife commits suicide. But she is not buried."

"Because she's a suicide," said Will.

"Right. Because back then, suicides would not have been buried in hallowed ground. She would have had to go somewhere else, maybe back on the Cottrell farm. But now comes the strange part. Two days later, Ephraim is dug up again and moved. But it doesn't say where. And it doesn't say who moved him."

Then I knew. In that moment it all came together. A story, like Pastor Hurd said, full of pain.

A man with enough money for three sawmills.

A man chosen as town selectman.

Two weathered stones with no names in the Emerson Burial Yard.

"It was Hieronymous Emerson," I said. "Hieronymous had the money. He could have paid Ephraim Cottrell three hundred dollars to go in his place. But when he was killed at Antietam, Hieronymous brought his body back, maybe because he felt that Ephraim had died in his place." ("We owe it to them," Grandma had said.)

"It fits," said Pastor Hurd. "But what about the missing bodies?"

"There are two stones side by side in the Emerson Burial Yard apart from the rest of the family. They must be

Ephraim and Charity Cottrell. Hieronymous was probably as cantankerous as Grandpa. When the church wouldn't bury Charity, he did. And then he brought Ephraim from the churchyard to lie side by side with her."

Pastor Hurd looked back at the records. "Maybe what you say is what happened. It does all fit. It leaves Erastus out, though."

"No, they took him in. He's listed in the family Bible."

Pastor Hurd closed the records. "Imagine what it would have been like. A man is killed in your place. You bring him back to bury him—out of guilt—but that only leads to the wife's death. A heavy burden to carry. So you take in the son—out of guilt. Every time you look at him you see him accusing you of killing his parents, and you have to care for him because his accusation is just."

It was a story full of power.

We left the church at late dusk with a tale worth telling for our report. A wave at the parsonage door and I was biking home on clear roads whose shoulders bulged with snow. There was still one part of the story that didn't fit: the Sin Eater. For Hieronymous to have buried him in the Emerson graveyard, he must have had some connection. And maybe it wasn't a coincidence that his stone was close to the Cottrells. He had written that he had one thing left to do. Maybe that one thing had something to do with Hieronymous. Or with the Cottrells. Or maybe he never had a chance to do it. Or maybe he really was buried there out of gratitude for saving the Emerson children from the fever.

When I got home, a light mizzle rain had started to fall.

It rained that way for the whole week up to Christmas.

145

The sky hung down just over the fields and dripped and drizzled. In two days the snow was gone. In three days it looked as if all the color in the world had drained away.

When the fields are covered with snow, everything is sharp—the green of the pines, the blue of the spruces, the flash of the blue jay, the changing light of a sunset. But in a drizzle, everything fades into itself. The grass was a rotting, dank green, the bare branches a dark wet, and everywhere there was mud. It squelched out from your boots as you stepped, it climbed up onto the shanks of Nutmeg and Cinnamon, it spread in a stain across the kitchen linoleum where we walked. It got so that The Frisian wouldn't go out in the fields, not if it meant getting all his feathery fettles dirty.

By Christmas Eve standing water filled the vegetable garden and overflowed onto the grassy borders. The woodstove kept everything in the house dry, but from the milk shed on back it felt as if you could wring out the air. Grandpa fussed about the hay starting to get moldy with the damp.

But towards late morning a cold wind started to come down as if the White Mountains were shredding the clouds and *shooshing* them out to sea. "I never did see the mercury drop as fast as this," Grandpa observed, looking out the window. "Best to get in another armload of wood, Cole."

Out in the barn, the animals felt the new front; the Frisian stood perfectly still in his stall against the coming cold. I gathered stove-length sticks enough to last until supper and carried them back through the sheds, shivering. I could see my breath right up until the kitchen.

146

In the best room Grandpa was reading from a pile of old letters his brother had written to their mother during World War II, adorned with French postmarks. Grandma was hottening cider and flavoring it with a vanilla bean. The apple and vanilla smell filled the air, overpowering the hot, dry scent of the woodstove. It's been this way for 150 years, I thought suddenly. I could be Erastus walking in here, with wood, and the world would be nothing different.

By the time we drove to the Christmas Eve service, the sky was free of clouds and the air so cold it squinted my eyes. I breathed in the wet wool of the scarf, thinking about the piles of Christmas bulbs left by the tree, waiting until we got back. I'd left my presents behind the tree. For Dad, a collection of thick winter socks. (I didn't want to get him anything bigger because I was pretty sure he hadn't gotten me anything and I didn't want to embarrass him.) For Grandma, a map of New England so old that it showed New Hampshire as running into Vermont. And for Grandpa, a used case knife I'd found at Roy Lanier's Hardware. I'd cleaned all the rust away and oiled the hinges so that the four blades sprang up at a touch.

Miss Cottrell must have found the candles—"No thanks to Pastor Hurd"—because she had filled the church with them. Their flames flickered with the drafts, trembling the light. But they made us all quiet and thoughtful. "Infant holy, Infant lowly," we all sang as if it were a lullaby and we were cajoling a baby to sleep. Kaye sang "I Wonder as I Wander" as the candles warmed the air and scented it like honey. Then Will got up to recite the Christmas story.

He did it simply, as if he was only telling us a story about

147

something he had seen and remembered. He kept his hands in his back pockets, except once when he tried to loosen his tie, which had a stranglehold on him. He told of the rude innkeeper, the hasty arrangements, and the baby amid all the confusion and muck. And when he finished, I saw Mrs. Dowdle wipe her eyes.

"Hark the Herald Angels Sing" next, then Pastor Hurd's meditation—short since the wind was picking up and it was rattling all the loose panes in the church—and then "Silent Night, Holy Night" and we were out into the cold.

"A Merry Christmas to you," called Mr. Cooper. "It'll be a cold one."

Grandma waved back. Her scarf muffled her face and she wasn't going to take it off simply to call back to Mr. Cooper.

"Merry Christmas to you too," Grandpa hollered, and then, in a voice he thought no one heard, "you old fool." Someone, probably Will, began ringing the bronze bells of the church, and their sweet song sang against the chill.

The kitchen was cold when we got home.

"You'd think he could—"

"Hiram . . ." Grandma warned, touching his shoulder, and Grandpa quieted right down.

"You fetch the wood, Cole, and I'll stoke it up," Grandpa suggested. I went out to the barn, turning the lights on in the shed and then off as I left. I checked to see if any of the animals were kneeling—they weren't—and then counted out enough of a load to get the woodstove blazing. And it didn't take long; the chimney was still warm and the draft pulled right up.

In the front room Grandma slid some Christmas carols

onto the phonograph. She brought out the pitcher of egg-nog with four cups, and while Grandpa and I started to open the boxes, she poured.

"My grandmother used to make this same recipe when I was a girl," she said. "We'd have it every Christmas Eve after church, with cookies made with the best of the year's maple syrup."

"Your Ma, Cole, she was the one who could make eggnog," said Grandpa. "That was her job alone, that and putting the angel on the tip, tip top of the tree."

"I remember that," I said. "I remember Ma putting the angel on once."

Grandpa nodded, remembering. "If she were here, she would be the one to do it."

We were all quiet a long time while the wind pushed at the house and whined because it could not get in.

"Well, I won't stand to see us get all melancholy on Christmas Eve." Grandma stood suddenly, hands on hips. "I'm going to get your father, Cole. He should be here for this. You two start hanging the balls. Remember to put those heavy ones farther inside. And if the threads are too short there's some in that basket underneath the window." She marched off on her mission.

Grandpa smiled and shook his head. "You never have to ask why I married her, do you?" He drained his eggnog as I hung the first bulb on the Christmas tree, a glass star.

A sudden clatter of feet down the stairs, and a door thrown open against a wall. A stifled cry, then a choke. Something shattering against the floor.

Grandpa and I ran into the kitchen, pushing against each other. Grandma stood at the bottom of the stairway to the hired man's room, her eyes wide and frantic, her mouth open but no sound coming out. Her hands were red, and with them she pointed to the stairs.

Grandpa sprinted up, and when I tried to follow, Grandma grabbed me by the shoulders and pressed me to her, tight against her chest, her hands gripping my shoulder blades as if to keep me from flying apart.

I looked past her shoulders across the kitchen. The gun rack over the door was empty.

NINE

On Christmas Day a cold front swept down from across a thousand miles of the North Atlantic, bringing the smell of the whitecaps far inland and sleeting the streets, the houses, the fields until there was an inch and a half of ice across everything. The trees were thick with glazing, and their branches lay around them, having shattered to the ground and skittered their encasements like crystal. A dust of snow in late afternoon hid the ice storm, but no car could move.

Christmas services at Albion Grace Church of the Holy Open Bible were canceled. No one could possibly get to the church, and besides, Pastor Hurd had us to attend to.

He must have gotten the news sometime early in the morning. Probably the sheriff had stopped on his way up to our farm. But then again, Pastor Hurd might have still been awake, the Christmas carols still in his ear, when on this Holy Night of the year the tale of another suicide had come to be registered in the church records.

The sheriff was a cautious man; last night he had put chains on his tires before driving out. The ambulance hadn't and arrived first, its red light flashing and siren wailing out across the stricken world like a demon. Its light filled the yard and shone into the barn, so The Frisian started to put up a ruckus, and even Emily, Anne, and Charlotte set up a complaining mooing. Grandpa sent me in to calm them. I stroked their muzzles and let their warm breath play over my face. I poured out some grain for The Frisian. For the cows I ripped handfuls of fresh hay from the loft and fed it to them, and soon they were chewing happily. Nutmeg and Cinnamon, bedded down against the cold, just nuzzled into each other and slept.

Somehow the chores kept the white emptiness of the world from blowing in and blotting me out. If I could just not think, I could hold myself from the nothing that filled me with its hole and tried to push my guts down to my feet and my brain against my skull. I felt like I was about to throw up.

Outside, the red light turned off. I heard a door slam, the ambulance starting up, and then the whine of the tires spinning heatedly over the ice that was just then starting to lay itself down. "Don't crank it," hollered the sheriff. "Just take it slow." The ambulance moved off, crunching over the icy gravel of the driveway.

The cows were all down now, legs folded underneath

them, eyes mostly closed. I lay down beside the sweet warmth of Emily's body and pulled hay over me until I was mostly covered, the dry stalks pricking and scratching all over me while I settled in.

And that was how Grandpa found me. Asleep on the hay.

"You okay?" he asked.

"I guess."

His eyes dropped. "Sorry about what happened, Cole."

"So am I." It was all I could do to get the words out.

Grandpa hung his Coleman lantern on a nail, spread out a quilt he'd carried in, and sat down on it. He felt me watching him. "I'll stay by until morning," he said quietly. "Go back to sleep." So I settled down into the hay.

When I awoke, Grandpa had already started in on the chores. He mucked out while I spread feed, and then together we ran through the icy sleet of that Christmas morning across the yard and up the porch, past two sets of snowshoes propped against the clapboards.

By the time we got inside, we had sleet frozen in our hair.

Talk stopped as we came in the kitchen. Pastor Hurd stood up from the table, still holding a mug of coffee. Will stood with him. Grandma stopped mixing over the stove and stepped anxiously towards me, one hand holding the spatula, the other holding the iron fry pan with scrambled eggs. Everything seemed unusually clear that morning: the wisps of her hair that had escaped her net, the knit on the potholder that she'd wrapped around the handle, the tissue stuck up her sweater sleeve.

"Come have some breakfast," she said, in a voice

strained and quiet. I slid in between the table and the wall, next to Will, and Grandpa and Pastor Hurd sat down across from us.

"Cole," said Pastor Hurd, "Will and I, we're both very sorry about your father."

Grandma set down the plate of eggs and I began to eat them.

"It was never meant to be like this, Cole. Death was never meant to be a part of things."

I ate the eggs quickly, like an animal, and pushed the plate away.

"I know," I said to Pastor Hurd. "Things don't have to be the way they are. But just knowing that doesn't help much."

"No," he agreed, "it doesn't help much."

Grandpa nodded, turning his coffee mug in his hand.

"We never did get to that tree last night," I said.

"No," said Grandma quickly. "We never did."

Will and I spent most of the morning trimming the tree, as the ice storm glazed the windows and low voices spoke in the kitchen. We didn't talk hardly at all; we did what had to be done like a practiced team until lights glowed softly against the garland and bulbs. We stacked the empty boxes with their trailing tissue paper in the closets. Nothing more to be done.

Will left with Pastor Hurd after lunch, refusing Grandpa's offer of a ride. "Not on a day like this," Pastor Hurd said. "Anyway it looks like it'll turn to snow soon, and we'll stop at Mrs. Dowdle's to get warm."

"I'll call ahead to let her know you're coming."

"Thank you, Livia. That'll mean there'll be hot choco-late waiting for us." Then he turned to me. He didn't know

153

what to say. "Cole." A long pause. "You're in our prayers." Will punched me on the shoulder, softly, and then they were gone, clomping down the drive with their snowshoes. I watched them on the road, watched Will laugh as Pastor Hurd sat down hard on his rump. Watched as he tripped up Will so that he sat down beside him. Watched them laughing and trying to help each other up. Then I let the curtain fall across the window.

The house was very still. I went back to my room and slept until Grandma called me to supper.

Dinner was desperately normal. Emersons had had pork roasts for Christmases without number, laying them against apple sauce and roast potatoes. Dessert was Christmas cake, pasted with almond sauce. Christmas folded into Christmas, and I remembered times when I had laughed and sung over this same meal.

"I think I left the pork on too long."

"It's fine, Livia."

"Fine," I said.

"I suppose it's all right."

That was almost all we said that meal. Mostly we clattered dishes.

When Grandma began clearing away, Grandpa spoke about Dad. His hands had been fidgeting back and forth, until finally he clenched them together. "Cole, there's some things we'll need to decide about the funeral."

"Do you have a funeral story, Grandpa?"

"The family has been around a long time; there's lots of funeral stories."

"Tell one."

"Cole," said Grandpa.

"Go ahead and tell," said Grandma, sitting down.

"Now's not the time for telling stories."

"Maybe," Grandma said slowly, "there isn't any better time. Tell about Brewster."

At this Grandpa smiled and gave in. Maybe it was because he couldn't resist her asking, or because he couldn't resist telling a story. Or maybe he just wanted to fill up the empty silence. He leaned back in his chair.

"Hieronymous's son Brewster was a red-haired, fiery-tempered cuss who swore up and down all his life he wouldn't be a farmer. But he had three younger sisters and an older brother gone to sea, and he figured he couldn't get out of it. When he was seventeen years old, though, Erastus came to live with the family and Brewster saw his chance. One spring night he loaded a pack and set out for Quebec to be a trapper; the note he left was the last the family heard of him for years and years. Up to the day he died, Hieronymous never spoke of him again. But with his last breath, it was Brewster's name he called out. Lydia, Hieronymous's wife, your great-great grandmother, Cole, lived nine more years. In 1907, when spring was coming on, and everything was mud, she caught pneumonia. She settled down into her pillows and stayed in bed during daylight for the first time in her life. Her children and grandchildren took turns around her, but she was too weak to talk. Every so often she'd give a gentle cough, the only thing that told she was still alive.

"Late one night, when she was failing fast, the kitchen door opened suddenly and a stranger came in, smelling of wet and mud. He was pretty much lame and used a cane to get around. His hair was white, his face tanned like

155

leather. Everyone waiting in the kitchen thought it might be someone the doctor had sent out with some new medicine, so they led him into Lydia's bedroom.

"'Mama,' they whispered. 'Mama, it's someone here to see you. Can you open your eyes, Mama?' So she did. Wide and wider. She reached out a hand—it was hard for her to get it out from under the quilt—and the stranger knelt down and let her run it over his face.

"'You rascal,' she said to him. 'You missed your father.'

"The stranger nodded and placed his hand over hers, holding it to his cheek.

"'You almost missed me, but I waited.'

"'Thank you, Mama,' he said. 'You waited a long time.'

"She smiled at that. 'Time doesn't mean much,' she said. 'It's the waiting that counts.' It was the last thing she said. Her hand drooped and he tucked it under the quilt.

"At the funeral, Sophie and Betsy with their husbands, and Hannah and Erastus, and Brewster with them stood together on one side of the grave, the grandchildren behind them, the casket on the far side. The minister read through the service, and when he finished, the grand-children were supposed to come around and lower Lydia into the grave. But Sophie had been fuming all that time. Here's that brother, gone for half a century, and then he shows up with no explanation at all. She could hardly stand it anymore. At the last Amen, she leaned back and fetched Brewster's cane a kick, cracking it right in two. Brewster had been leaning on it, and when it snapped he fell for-ward, smack-dab in the open grave headfirst.

"Sophie threw her hands up to her face; she could hardly believe what she had done. The grandchildren all
156

stopped; they couldn't lower Lydia on top of Brewster. And the minister, well, he walked back into the house. He didn't want to be a part of what happened next.

"But what happened next maybe wasn't what he expected. Everyone was looking down into the grave, Uncle Brewster looking up. And suddenly the sides started to slosh in, mud giving way. Old Brewster, he struggled up, but the sides collapsed up to his knees, then his waist. Sophie's and Betsy's husbands reached in, but the sides just collapsed under them and ran into Brewster, who was by now up to his chest.

"Finally Erastus came back with a rope, threw one end over the casket and the other to Uncle Brewster, who tied it around his chest. Everyone who could get a hand on the rope pulled, but with the mud sucking at him the rope just tightened and tightened until he started to turn a kind of blue. 'Untie the knot,' they called to him, but by now it was so wet and tight no one could have untied it.

"They almost gave him up until Sophie came back with the plow horse and threw the reins down to him. 'Where should I tie them?' he asked.

"'Around your neck,' she hollered back.

"He tied them under his arms and she smacked the rump of the horse and he plucked him out like a cork, mud from his toes to his ears.

"Sophie came back and loosed the reins from him. 'Sister,' he said, 'you didn't mean to bury me, did you?'

"'It would be nothing less than you deserve.'

"'That's true enough,' he agreed. 'But Sophie, let's all hope that we don't get what we deserve.' At that Sophie threw her arms around his muddy self and cried and cried and cried. And he cried too, tears cleaning his cheeks, crying for Lydia, for Hieronymous, and for fifty years gone by.

"As far as I know, no one found out what Uncle Brewster had been doing for all that time, or how his leg got lame, or why he came back. Sophie and her family took him in, and he lived with them the rest of his life. Maybe he told them some stories, but if so, they never repeated them. If you look in the Emerson Burial Yard tomorrow, you can see that he's buried right beside Sophie, and you can see Lydia a piece away from Hieronymous, where they had to dig a new grave."

Grandpa, finished, sat back in his chair, looking at his hands. Grandma went to answer the whining of the tea kettle.

"A good story," I said.

"And it's mostly true. Or as true as any story ought to be."

"What did Lydia mean, it's the waiting that counts, and not the time?"

"I think it means that it isn't time that's so important, it's what you do with it." Grandpa coughed once, low. "That's true about your dad, too, Cole. Somehow he knew he didn't have much more time. So he tried to do something good with it: He brought you here to us. A good thing. And then your father waited as long as he could, and if it wasn't as long as you hoped, still, he did wait."

"You're right," I said. "It wasn't as long as I hoped."

Grandma brought mugs of tea back, and the steam curled into the air. "Do anything you like about the funeral," I said. "It doesn't matter much. At least with the ground frozen we can count on it not filling in. That's one story that won't repeat."

"No story ever repeats, Cole," said Grandpa.

"Then why bother remembering any of them?"

Grandpa looked right at me. "So we can know who we are. So we can share one another's lives, and somehow carry one another's lives. So we know how to live."

"Or how not to live," I said softly and left for bed. I slept in thickened darkness without moving all night.

The next day I lay in bed late, listening to the house. Downstairs Grandma pounded yeast dough, thrusting her fists into the mass and turning them—I could see her—over and over, then shaping the dough into proper rectangles. I heard Grandpa come in from the barn chores, slamming the door against the cold and dropping an armload of maple into the woodbox.

"Cold today, but the snow's let up." Grandpa's words came through the house. But I couldn't hear if Grandma answered or not.

They both had so much to do to fill their lives.

And me? I lay in bed, watching for the sheets of snow that the wind blew off the roof, listening to the whistling draft that edged in under the windowsills. I didn't get up until the rig came up from town to gash out a hole in the Emerson Burial Yard, right next to Ma's. I watched through the window, the claw piercing through the snow and ice and mixing it with the mess of dirt, staining the blue air with exhaust, clunking as the metal struck stone. When the rig left, Grandpa went out to shovel snow over the tracks and to set right one of the stones budged over.

When I came to breakfast the bread was out, warm and brown, and the yeast smell filled the kitchen. The air shimmered around the woodstove that was heaving heat against the cold of the day, and the sun was all in a rush through the windows, brightening up the green of the geraniums on the sills.

"There's waffles still warm in the oven, and syrup on the stove," Grandma said. She was up to her elbows in flour and dough, pounding and turning in her mixing bowl. "Your grandpa's outside"—a long pause—"seeing to things."

I ate all the waffles in the oven and another batch she cooked up, then headed out to the woods south of the farm.

The snow had piled up to a few inches above a light crust, so I cracked through every time I stepped down and threw a cloud every time I stepped out. But in the woods there was only a light dusting on the ground, so thick were the branches overhead. The pines had been logged when Grandpa was just a boy, and these trees had been set out in lines slanting upwards, so I walked as though down an aisle until they started to give way to the hardwoods.

And it was right there, when pine gave way to maple, that I saw the buck.

He stood watching me, black eyes staring without movement, tail high and rigid. He had eight points on him and he held his head high and cocky as if he knew it. His pelt was thick with the winter cold, and his right front leg was bent slightly, as if he had been pawing at something through the snow. In the frigid, bright air his breath came

160

out in steam from his nostrils. Suddenly a crow shook snow down from a hemlock tree and flew *cawing, cawing, cawing* above the trees. I took my eyes away for a second to watch the flight, and when I looked back the buck was bounding away in high arcs, pushing itself into the air with his flanks and threading zigzag through the trees. I followed at a run, the branches catching my coat and whipping at my face until the blood came. For a time I could hear him snapping branches, but soon I had only the tracks to follow. They spaced out for a hundred yards or so, then came together all in a bunch as the buck paused to catch his breath. Then they spaced out again, back and forth between the trees.

I followed the buck into the afternoon, circling through the woods, the spaces between tracks shortening as the shadows of the woods grew longer, until we came down to Mr. Cooper's farm and I stepped out from the trees.

The buck stood on the far side of Mr. Cooper's corn-stubble field, heading in towards the sun that had come down to the tree line and hung huge and orange. Looking back at me, his chest heaving in short, quick gasps, the head still high, the buck stood for a moment as the sun gilded its antlers like a halo in their brightness. Then he turned and spurted away into the pines.

I stood a long time, watching the pines tug the sun down further and further into their shadowy branches, the cold numbing me. Suddenly I held both hands up and waved them madly, waved them into the gathering darkness. Then I headed across the farm and up to the River Road that would take me back for supper. The white hole in my gut was still there, only filled a bit.

Grandpa and Grandma, who knew the value of silence, let me be during that whole evening.

The funeral the next day was quiet and still. I felt everyone watching me, like on that first day when Dad and I had walked down the aisle of Albion Grace Church of the Holy Open Bible. The church was still decorated for Christmas—candles and Sunday School banners and boughs and beeswax candles. The only thing that was missing was the manger scene up front; that had been replaced by the casket. Miss Cottrell had banked the poinsettias up against it and set a line of white candles across its closed top. I sat in the front pew between Grandpa and Grandma, their bodies wedged close to mine to hold me tight. Grandma was trembling and she held her handkerchief in her hand. Grandpa was rock still, his hands folded. I wondered if he was even blinking. Behind me I could hear people shuffling and some soft crying from Mrs. Dowdle, I think. A few kids who wanted to get back to their Christmas toys kept asking, When will this be over?

When would this be over? Suddenly I realized that someday all this too would be just a memory.

Pastor Hurd talked some and Kaye Cottrell sang some, but all I could do was stare at the four candles burning on the casket. Their flames never shook; they were as solid as if they were made of bright glass. Pastor Hurd never said anything about this being a suicide as far as I could tell, but the word hung in the air the whole service, and even I wondered what I would have seen if the casket were open.

Afterwards we all drove slowly back home to Grandpa's

farm and the Emerson Burial Yard. It wasn't so bitter cold as it had been, and the wind had died down so we could stand without slapping our sides. Someone had taken bright green carpet and laid it neatly around the grave to tidy things up, but we all stood in the packed-down snow. The casket lay suspended over the grave; the pile of dirt lay discreetly behind the oak. Will and Peter stood across the grave from me, blinking away the cold.

I kept feeling everyone's eyes on me, like they wanted me to say something, or fly into a panic, or just start to cry. But I didn't do any of these. I just stood there, quiet, holding Grandma's trembling hand, feeling Grandpa stand rigidly beside me, listening to Pastor Hurd's low voice, and trying hard to look at anything but the one thing I could not help but look at.

"Almighty and merciful Father," prayed Pastor Hurd. "You know the weakness of our nature. Bow down your ear in pity upon your servants, upon whom lays the heavy burden of sorrow. Teach them to see the good and gracious purpose working in all trials which you send to them. Grant that they do not languish in fruitless grief, nor sorrow as those do who have no hope. But in their tears, have them look up meekly to you, the God of consolation. Through Christ our Lord. Amen."

I expected that people would start to leave then and we would get on with the business of the day. Afternoon chores were coming up, and I had heard The Frisian neigh impatiently twice since it was past time for his grain. But no one moved. We all stood there in the lowering light, still except for the occasional pickup that drove by and slowed down to see what was going on, still except for a blue jay that crackled through the bare branches.

Then Kaye started to sing.

It was a hum at first, as quiet as the snowy fields around us, until she got to the middle of the song.

> *"When I fall on my knees,*
> *With my face to the rising sun,*
> *O Lord, have mercy on me."*

The second time through everyone sang but Grandma and Grandpa and me. And the third time even Grandma joined in, her voice high and quavery. And when the last notes died down people finally started to move off, coming up one by one to shake Grandpa's hand and to pat me on the shoulder. Grandma went inside to help organize the baskets of food that people brought for our supper that night. Will, Peter, and I ran into the barn to quick feed The Frisian and quiet him down. Will stroked his muzzle while Peter fed the goats and I shoved hay in front of the cows. When we came out, cars were starting in the driveway, their exhaust rising in the cold air like fog and the smell of it thick.

The Gealys were standing outside their car, waiting for Peter. The two girls were already in the backseat under a checked blanket, their faces pressed against the rear window, watching for their brother. I walked with Peter over to the car. "See you in school," he said, and looked long at me before he got in.

Mr. Gealy shook my hand. "You come down anytime, Cole."

And Mrs. Gealy. Well, Mrs. Gealy didn't say anything. But she kissed me again on the forehead, and that was enough. When they drove away, I almost cried. It would have been the first time that day.

Back in the Emerson Burial Yard, the casket had been lowered down and two men I had never seen before were shoveling in the dirt. I tried not to listen to the hollow sound.

Will and I went to stand by Grandpa and Pastor Hurd, and we all were quiet until the grave was filled in and mounded over; the men worked expertly, like landscapers. And when they were finished and had rolled up the bright green carpet and piled their gear into the pickup waiting by the road, Grandpa turned to Pastor Hurd and spoke for the first time that day that I had heard.

"So where is God in all of this?" His words were fierce, a growl.

The wind started to kick up then, shedding snow over the dark mound. I watched it gather.

"Hiram," answered Pastor Hurd finally, "God is in mourning."

A short, gutteral gasp jolted out of Grandpa. A single tear wiped hastily away. Then, firmly, a handshake and Grandpa stalking into the house.

Grandpa never put together another List of Theological Errors, at least none that ever found its way to Pastor Hurd. When Grandma asked why the change of heart, he told her that Pastor Hurd had the most important thing down, and after that the lists didn't matter much.

What Grandpa meant by the most important thing I

didn't know then. I suppose there was a story mixed up in there somewhere.

But that night when I went to bed, I didn't think of stories, or Dad, or Ma, or even the day.

I thought of the Sin Eater and wondered if the anger in my soul was something that he could ever have taken away. Or if I would even have wanted him to.

TEN

Right about the time when Grandpa's father took over the farm, around 1893 or so, a series of cold winters flew down to New Hampshire that people in Albion still talk about. The first frost crept out to the fields and into the gardens sometime right after the first of September, turning the tomato leaves black and wilting all the flowers overnight. The corn stiffened and dried; the lilac leaves turned so hard that it seemed they would shatter when they fell.

By the end of the month the first snows came on, and they stayed longer than they had any right to. The ground held white past April. In May the snow turned into rocky ice and finally melted off by the end of the month. But the nights brought frost well into June.

It wasn't what you would call a long planting season.

People around Albion thought that Bertram Emerson, Grandpa's father, was an impatient man. They could probably tell it simply by watching him prowl around his fields towards the end of April or by watching him in the barn,

166

the harnesses and machinery oiled and all set to haul out to plow, but then having to sit there until the melt. Every morning he'd go out to his fields, his hands above his eyes against the glare of the snow, and he'd use words that he wasn't allowed to use in the house. Spring after spring he waited past what he should have had to wait, watching the snow slowly melt, waiting for the last signs of frost to disappear from the skies.

For an impatient man, it was a hard time.

When the spring of 1897 looked like it was going to be as cold and frosty as all the rest of that decade, Bertram Emerson figured that fair is fair, and he wasn't going to put up with frost into June anymore. Not even in New Hampshire. At the end of May, when the ground was still icy-white, Bertram hitched the team up and plowed, scooting the dirt and ice together in furrowed heaps, white and black under the cold sun. He plowed up the vegetable garden, and then the kitchen garden. And after that he plowed up another forty acres that had lain fallow for two or three years, just for good measure.

When he was done, he set in to plant.

He put in fifty acres of corn, then fifty of summer wheat. In the new forty he planted alfalfa. In the vegetable garden he planted sweet corn, the plants taken from the cold frame and put naked into the snow and earth. He held off on planting the tomatoes, but butter beans, pole beans, sweet peas, Dutch onions, and supersweet carrots all took their places, the frost hanging in the soil beneath and above them.

Bertram planted with his thick gloves on, a scarf around his neck and over his ears—which was just as well, since he didn't hear his neighbors guffawing as they rode by, taking advantage of the late snow to slide in an extra load of firewood logs. And his rows weren't straight, since he had to keep his eyes mostly shut against the sunlight coming off the ice. But by the first week of June everything was in and Bertram brought the gleaming plow back into the barn.

Everyone in Albion knew that he would have it all to do over again.

But he didn't.

Just about the time when Bertram started plowing, warm winds began to blow up from the Connecticut valleys, blossoming out the apple trees two weeks early. They headed across into Massachusetts, greening things as they came, setting the bees to going and the caterpillars to building cocoons. At the New Hampshire border they paused a day or so, not quite sure whether it was their time or not, but finally shrugged their shoulders and headed to Albion, greening and blossoming and turning the air yellow. A day or so after Bertram finished planting, the winds arrived and warmed everything to mud.

No one could plant then; they had to wait until things dried before they could drive a plow through. But Bertram, he went out into his fields every day just to pace down the rows of green shoots that were sucking the sun and the water up just as fast as they could.

His crops stayed three weeks ahead of everyone else's that summer; his was the only corn to reach knee-high by the Fourth of July. And when the first frost came on September 3, he had his crops harvested, the only one in Portsmouth County.

From then on, folks planted whenever Bertram Emerson planted. It was quite a responsibility, being a prophet more honored than *The Farmer's Almanac*. When he walked by, people would wag their heads at him. "Bertram Emerson," they'd say. "He can plant in the snow."

And that's what Grandma and Grandpa were doing most of the winter that year for me: planting in the snow.

For Grandma, planting meant apple pies and cinnamon rolls and sweet yams and pole beans steeped in buttery milk. Between all the cooking she tore off the wallpaper in the hired man's room and pulled up the linoleum. She did this while I was at school. I only found out because I saw it in the canisters in the back shed.

For Grandpa, planting meant stories. He told about Ma learning how to swim at Coffin Pond—"Damnedest name I ever heard of for a swimming pond," he said. And he talked about the first time she'd gone to a farm auction with him in Brunswick and how they somehow bought a weather vane, a lightning rod, and a broad axe. "We didn't need a single one of them, but there she sat behind me holding up her hand just 'cause she'd got it into her head that she wanted those things."

The weather vane and lightning rod are up on the barn now. The broad axe is hanging in the toolshed, polished and oiled against rust in case any of us ever comes across a beam that needs squaring.

Grandpa didn't have any stories about Dad. Not a one.

And the thing was, neither did I.

With Ma, I could see a plot of tulips, or hear Miss Bradshaw pitch a hymn in the low notes, or smell gingerbread, and she would be right there. Right there.

Tulips sprouting bright yellow and dusty red, their green fronds full and wet and her laughing in the spring light to see her fall work fill the front of the porch with color.

Her standing at the church front, ready to sing "How Firm a Foundation," and Miss Bradshaw plunging the key down basement level, so that even my father would have had a rough time with it.

Me eating a dozen hot gingerbread men before Ma even got to frost them, and feeling them warm and clumpy in my stomach. And Ma coming in, mixing a bowl of almond frosting and swatting me out of the kitchen. And me coming back in to help make a new batch, the smell of the gingerbread everywhere.

But for Dad, there was nothing. No stories. Nothing.

Late January locked down the Great Hosmer, so whenever Will and Peter and I didn't have a driveway or sidewalk to shovel, we'd skate on the lake's green ice. Will skated easy, with his arms behind his back, never catching a toe, never missing an edge going backwards or forwards. Peter looked like he was racing, leaning his chest over on the air.

Me, I skated straight up and down like a board, more interested in staying up than anything else. But that's what made skating so good. When I was skating, I couldn't think of anything but skating. First one foot, now the next, the vibration of the glide coming up through the edge to my ankles and knees and into my guts, watching for the cracks or the holes left by ice fishermen. We skated until the sun glowed red and it was a chore to lift our legs. Then, numb, we'd glide to shore and pick at the frozen laces until they gave.

Once home, chores and homework and eating and sleep.

And so I slipped, numb and asleep, through the winter, as the snows piled up on two graves outside, and as the stories of Ma came less frequently and those of Dad stayed buried with him.

Even Grandpa and Grandma stopped telling the stories. I suppose they thought that stories hurt too much. They did.

It was right around this time that Miss Cottrell stepped outside one night to look at the stars and never made it home.

Later we supposed that she wanted to get away from the lights of the town and so headed out to River Road. And the farther away she got, the clearer and brighter the stars. But also the farther away from home.

It was Mrs. Dowdle who got up for her four o'clock cordial and noticed that all of Miss Cottrell's lights were still on. When she did not answer her phone, Mrs. Dowdle called the sheriff. By morning he had a search organized, stretched out between the Commons and our farm. Just at breakfast he came to the top of Cobb's Hill and told Grandpa and me about Miss Cottrell when we came out to see why cars had lined up along our garden. And before he finished telling, Peter was biking up. Will and Pastor Hurd were starting the search at the bottom of River Road, the sheriff said. Perhaps Peter and I could start at the top of Cobb's Hill.

I shivered by the warm black-and-white while Grandpa explained how the woods went and where they might start looking. Mr. Fordham held a topographical map, and with a red pencil he blocked out the area he assigned to the deputies. But the whole time he was shaking his head. "Mr. Emerson, last night being as cold as it was, you know what the chances are."

Grandpa turned and looked at me before he spoke to the sheriff. "Stubborn old cusses don't give in all that easily. And I expect that within the hour you'll have half of Albion Grace Church of the Holy Open Bible praying for Miss Cottrell. I've seen a lot worse chances than this."

The sheriff raised his eyebrows and turned back to his map.

"You, Cole," called Grandpa. "How well do you know these woods?"

"Enough not to get turned around."

Grandpa eyed me at that. Then he took off his gloves, dug around in his pocket, and handed me the knife I had given him for Christmas. "Take it. You never know when a knife will come in handy. And take the thermos too. Head on straight over to Cobb's Hill there. Maybe Miss Cottrell decided she'd just as soon walk on home and wanted a shortcut."

I nodded and Peter and I started off.

"And, Cole," he called once more, "check out the sugar maple cabin on the way."

The cabin was a quarter mile west of Cobb's Hill, in a small but steep valley. Erastus had set it there because he could run the maple sap in troughs right down the hill-

172

sides to a collector and then boil and boil and boil it to syrup. The troughs and most of the sugar maples were all gone, but Erastus built things to stay, and the cabin still had sound cedar shingles on its roof and sides. On a night like last night it wouldn't have been warm, but it would have been as dry as the day it was first set up—barring the one corner where the chimney had come away some.

In the woods, the snow was dry and powdery. I thought of Miss Cottrell stomping through here with her cane, starting to panic a bit when she lost her direction, maybe finding the cabin and settling in to wait, cold in a corner. "Miss Cottrell!" we hollered. "Miss Cottrell!" The calls of the sheriff came back to us, but by the time we reached the cabin everything was still as death; the only sounds were our feet crushing the snow and our own ragged breathing, shallow so as not to take the cold in too deep.

Will had shown me the cabin once and we had even talked about trying to tap some of the trees ourselves. It set in a grove of new-growth aspens and birch, its gray and weathered shingles fading into the forest. Old stumps stood around like squatting dwarves, the remains of the trees that Erastus had cut for the maple syrup fires. The door and two windows were on the side facing up the hill so that Erastus could watch the sap flow, but it meant that as we trudged up to it we couldn't tell if anyone had been there recently.

"Miss Cottrell!" No answer.

We went around to the front and jerked at the door, figuring that the settling of the cabin would have made it tight. But it gave easily, and Peter pulled it open.

Almost no light came through the windows, but something in the corner moved back behind the pile of sap buckets that Erastus had left.

"Miss Cottrell?"

We stepped closer.

"Miss Cottrell? It's me, Cole Hallet. Mr. Emerson's grandson. We've come for you."

A fierce snarling, then something bursting out from the pails, clunking them to the floor and brushing past us all in a furry rush out the door. I suppose I screamed or something; I know I found myself up on top of a barrel and my breath coming so fast it was racing my heart. "Damn," I breathed into the empty cabin. "Damn."

"I suppose that wasn't Miss Cottrell after all," Peter said.

I was breathing so hard that it took me a moment to answer. "I suppose not."

And then, standing on a barrel in the sap house of Erastus Emerson, I suddenly did know where Miss Cottrell was.

"Peter, when you came up today, Cobb's Hill was all ice, wasn't it?"

"As icy as all get-out."

I didn't need to finish. We ran outside the sap house and sprinted back, running as if some animal was clicking his teeth behind us. We were winded by the time we reached the top of the hill, where the sheriff had his map spread out over the hood of the black-and-white and Grandpa was still pointing out likely areas, marking them with a pencil. "You boys should have been to the sap house by now," Mr. Fordham called, annoyed, but we didn't answer.

We started down the hill, slip-sliding all the way to the pine grove at the bottom where the low branches of the pines hid the trunks from the road. All the patrol cars were parked down here, some with their lights still flashing. But when we went through the branches, none of that light reached in to flash on the snow covered with a layer of needles. Nor did it touch Miss Cottrell, who lay hunched up against a tree trunk, her right leg at an impossible angle.

Peter ran out to the road, holding on to the branches to keep himself from falling. "She's here," he called. "Down here. Here."

"Miss Cottrell," I whispered, close to her face. "Miss Cottrell."

And slowly she opened her eyes.

"Aren't you Hiram Emerson's boy?"

"His grandson."

She nodded once and closed her eyes. "It took you a long enough time to get here."

Then the branches parted and Peter came back in under the trees, his breath fierce.

"And a Gealy," said Miss Cottrell in short gasps. "An Emerson and a Gealy. Well, that makes it just right."

"Just right, Miss Cottrell?" The sheriff rushed in, one side of his jacket wet from where he had slid down, and soon it was all uniforms under the pines.

Supper that night was filled with Miss Cottrel.

"Imagine," said Grandma. "Here we are, all asleep, and at the bottom of the hill Miss Cottrell is lying in the snow with a broken leg."

Grandpa shook his head back and forth. "If it had been

a colder night, or snowy . . ." He left the consequences unspoken. "Still and all it's a fact that up in New Hampshire we don't get old and frail; we get old and tough."

"Some," suggested Grandma, "get tougher than others."

No answer from Grandpa on this.

"Why do you think Miss Cottrell said it was just right that an Emerson and a Gealy found her?" I'd been thinking on this since she had been handed into the ambulance.

Grandma got up and started to clear. "I expect she was just glad to see you boys."

"It was more than that though. There was a reason for it being just right that it was Peter and me that found her. And she didn't say Peter and Cole. She said an Emerson and a Gealy."

Grandpa thought for a bit, then pushed himself back from the table. "Well, maybe it's something you can ask her when we visit tomorrow night."

So I did. She was on the fourth floor of Portsmouth County Medical Center, fussing with the first remote she had ever used. "It keeps changing channels," she complained as Grandpa and I walked in. "I just touch it and it's on a new station."

"Maybe you're hitting the wrong button."

"I am not hitting the wrong button. All I do is jiggle it and—there, do you see? It's changed channels again."

"Because you hit a button."

"Hiram Emerson, I know when I hit a button and when I don't. Turn the fool thing off, Cole, and remove your hat. Now listen. Have you been to salt my sidewalk? I don't want anyone to slip on it."

"Yes," I said.

"My driveway?"

"Yes."

"And my mail? Who's collecting my mail? I don't want that Mrs. Dowdle doing it because she'll steam all the letters open to find out my business so it would be much better if Pastor Hurd or perhaps his son could collect my mail until—"

"Will Hurd is picking it up," interrupted Grandpa.

"Miss Cottrell," I asked, "why was it just right that a Gealy and an Emerson found you yesterday?"

"Who said that?"

"You did, after we found you."

"Well, I suppose it was just right." She sat up to flounce her pillows a bit, then settled back in. "A long time ago a Gealy brought a Cottrell to an Emerson; this time around, an Emerson brought a Gealy to a Cottrell."

"How long ago?"

"Before either Hiram or I can remember. It was in Thomas Gealy's time."

"The Sin Eater."

"Some called him that. When his farm burned down he moved up to your place, Hiram, and helped out Hieronymous."

"Yes," nodded Grandpa, "we knew that."

Miss Cottrell adjusted herself on the bed. She liked to keep us waiting on her.

"It wasn't long at all until he saw that something was wrong up there. Erastus Cottrell lived there, since he had nowhere else to go, but when he looked at Hieronymous he saw the man he blamed for killing his parents, and he

177

hated him. And every time Hieronymous saw the hate in those eyes he was reminded that he paid a man to go die for him. But Erastus couldn't say anything to Hieronymous, since he was treating him like his own—as much as he could—and Hieronymous couldn't say anything to Erastus, since it wasn't the boy's fault that his father had gone as a substitute."

"But the Sin Eater had nothing to do with that," I said.

Miss Cottrell snorted. "Don't interrupt. One day after a summer haying, Thomas Gealy sat down between Hieronymous and Erastus underneath the field oaks and asked Hieronymous to tell him about Grace."

"His daughter," Grandpa explained. "She died of fever when she was only three and was buried, the first Emerson in the burial yard."

"Just so," said Miss Cottrell. "And Hieronymous told him as much as he could before he couldn't say another word, what with his almost seeing her dancing on his knee. His eyes filled up with the memory of her. And when he was done, Thomas Gealy turned to Erastus and asked him about his parents, who were also buried in the Emerson Burial Yard. And Erastus, he told all that he remembered, up to the day when his mother left him at the Emerson farm, until his throat choked off. Then Thomas Gealy left them both sitting beneath the tree, and it was as if he carried away all that pain with him, and they fell into each other's arms like the two wounded souls they were.

"It's not time for more blood. I've a broken bone, not a blood disease. Take your needle and prick someone else."

This last was directed at a nurse, who stood helpless and

flabbergasted by the foot of Miss Cottrell's bed. I went to the window and looked at the darkened valley. Not a single light shone.

This was the last thing the Sin Eater had to do. I was sure of it. But there was one more thing.

"Miss Cottrell?" The nurse had won and Miss Cottrell was sitting tight-lipped, her arm outstretched beneath the needle. "Is that why the Sin Eater is buried up at the Emerson graveyard?"

The nurse plucked the needle out and put a Band-Aid on the drop of blood that formed. Miss Cottrell rubbed her hand back and forth over it.

"Well, there was a whole lot of trouble in the church over burying him; the minister even left when the church voted not to bury him in the church graveyard, him being a Sin Eater. But I expect that Hieronymous Emerson had already decided where he would be buried.

"After all, what else can you give," she asked, "to someone who teaches your house to love?"

That's all I ever learned about the Sin Eater. Stories and bits of stories, scattered around Albion like wisps of dandelions, as unconnected as the few letters still left on the Sin Eater's gravestone. And some day, when the stories are gone, the only thing left will be the gravestone, and no one will know its story.

Spring was late again that year; Bertram wouldn't have been surprised. When the frost finally came out of the ground in early April, it started to rain. And rain. And rain. Soon the water was standing in places it had no right to stand, so Mr. Cooper knew that it would be touch and go with his summer wheat this year, even with his new tractor.

Miss Cottrell was back home, leaning a bit more on her cane, but ready to fuss at Pastor Hurd about the pews up towards the church front needing a new stain. Which they did. One Sunday morning, Mrs. Dowdle stood up after the service and said to no one in particular that there was nothing in the Bible that said you ought to suffer during a long sermon and that some church committee should begin to see to some pew cushions, especially since it was well known that a body couldn't even bring a sofa pillow to sit on.

Miss Cottrell had the bushes around her house to fuss about. It hadn't been a hard winter but it had been a long one, and last year's oak leaves had wedged themselves into her spruces and yews so tightly they seemed part of the bush. Miss Cottrell wanted every one out. Every one. So Peter and Will and I, now open as Spring Yard Constructors, Inc., spent afternoons there for a week and a half, raking and gathering leaves and clipping hedges, careful not to mark Grandpa's paint job on the wrought iron. Miss Cottrell watched from the front porch window the whole time.

It was good to work with them. They were always the same. After last Christmas, everyone else at school had looked at me like I was diseased, some poor dog that needed to be put out of its misery. At church people touched me lightly and spoke quietly and said in weepy voices how sorry they were, though I didn't see why they should be sorry.

But with Will and Peter things were what they were. They didn't need to say anything about Dad because they knew there was nothing to say. Or at least nothing that I wanted to hear.

If I had been sprung full grown out of the earth, or if I had never known my father, it would have been about the same to me.

The first truly warm day came on the first Sunday in May. It was the kind of day when tulips perk up their leaves and straighten their swelling buds, when dandelions open up in riots, when the maples show off their shiny emerald finery, and fruit trees gush out in dainty pink. It was the kind of day when you knew that spring had really and truly come and summer was treading on its heels.

The doors and windows of Albion Grace Church of the Holy Open Bible were open to the new air, and it rushed into the church foyer and shook the ceiling cobwebs and snuck under Sunday School papers tacked to bulletin boards and blew winter dust from the lights.

In the sanctuary, I sat in the usual spot by Grandma and Grandpa, close to the front. Every time an usher walked past, he seemed scented with the spring air. All the kids in the congregation were asquiggle with it, and their parents seemed too taken with the spring to still them. Even Grandma and Grandpa turned and whispered loudly to pew neighbors.

Mrs. Dowdle was ushered by; she boldly held a sofa cushion under her arm. It was communion Sunday, and even though the sermon would be shorter, she intended to be comfortable.

Then a deacon came in, carrying six loaves of fresh

181

bread—probably Miss Cottrell's—and set them on the front table. Instantly the smell of the warm bread mingled with the spring air, and the two filled the sanctuary so you could hardly tell if you were breathing or tasting.

It was the same for everyone in the church, and I watched them all open their mouths to the air. There sat Mrs. Dowdle proudly on her cushion. And there Miss Cottrell straightening the table linen before the service began. And there Pastor Hurd coming in, his robes swishing, his eye searching out Mrs. Hurd and Will. And there Mr. Cooper, sitting like he was already up in his John Deere, which he probably would be if it wasn't Sunday.

Grandpa leaned over to whisper to Grandma. "Remember canning last summer's tomatoes?" he asked, and Grandma quickly stuffed her white-gloved hand into her mouth to keep from laughing out loud.

"Or you driving back from the County Fair," she answered in a moment.

"You mean with those two goats."

"Hiram, you know very well what I mean," and then it was Grandpa with his hand in his mouth.

"Though of course," continued Grandma, "that doesn't compare with the time you came inside after the outhouse covered with . . ."

"Olivia Emerson, you are in church."

And at that they both had to laugh out loud, drawing the eye of Pastor Hurd, who could do nothing on a spring day like this but smile.

The smell of the warm bread grew stronger, and suddenly I thought of the Sin Eater, coming to find a life in New Hampshire and finding more wounded people who needed him to listen. I thought of him under the field oaks, sitting between Hieronymous Emerson and Erastus Cottrell and listening to all the hurt and anger until it was no longer theirs but somehow his.

"What can you give to someone who teaches your house to love?"

You can hold on to the stories. You can remember them, and in remembering . . .

And suddenly it was no longer Hieronymous and Erastus and the Sin Eater under the trees, but Ma, Dad, and me, Dad tossing a rope over a branch and sending a slipknot up tight for a swing. And Ma laughing when Dad tested it and she had to help him stand after the branch came crashing down.

And there was Dad building pine bookshelves in my room, the whole room smelling of the raw lumber, and Dad building in a secret compartment that only he and I knew about.

And Dad trying to water-ski and falling sixteen times before he got the knack of it. And the time we hit a patch of ice on a toboggan ride and Dad rolled off with me before the toboggan smashed into a tree, and us breathing hard together in the snow, his arms tight around me.

And the time he held me when the red lights were flashing farther and farther down the street, out of our lives, and he wept hot tears that fell into my hair.

And how, a year later, we drove to the Catskills to watch the rising sun together, hand in hand, and how it hit us full and sudden.

The stories came in such a flood, such a flood that I couldn't stop them, while the smell of the bread grew stronger and stronger. The congregation rose to sing the first hymn, and all of our stories came together for one sharp moment.

I sat, my face in my hands, crying and crying and crying in Grace Church for the stories, for Ma, and for Dad, who once was lost but now was found.